Edward Burnaby Greene

The Satires of Juvenal Paraphrastically Imitated and Adapted to the Times

Edward Burnaby Greene

The Satires of Juvenal Paraphrastically Imitated and Adapted to the Times

ISBN/EAN: 9783337375171

Printed in Europe, USA, Canada, Australia, Japan

Cover: Foto ©Andreas Hilbeck / pixelio.de

More available books at **www.hansebooks.com**

THE

SATIRES

OF

JUVENAL

PARAPHRASTICALLY IMITATED,

And adapted to the TIMES.

WITH

A PREFACE.

Dupe to no Party's Rage, the gen'rous Mufe
Guilt in all Ranks dares honeftly accufe;
Nor Slave to Sect, nor fearful of Control,
She fpeaks the genuine Dictates of her Soul.

LONDON:
Printed for J. RIDLEY in St. James's Street.
MDCCLXIII.

PREFACE.

I PROPOSE not to enquire what species of satire would be most conducive to reform the manners of mankind, being inclined to think that satire has rarely done any essential good. If we take the Horatian way; the attempt to laugh people out of their vices will be found, I am apprehensive, not a little deficient to answer the end proposed; the only end to which it can be subservient being to exercise a wanton indiscriminate spirit of ridicule, tending rather, as indeed generally design'd, to shew the wit of the satirist, than the means of the delinquent's reformation.

To

To prove more fully the inefficacy of this vehicle of reproof, it may be considered, that vice being a violent difeafe requires a more violent remedy; the fons of corruption muſt have their wounds very deeply probed, or they break out in a ſhort time with redoubled fury; and as for thoſe of folly, they are earlieſt themſelves at the laugh, or at beſt ſit with all poſſible calmneſs and compoſure to ſee their own deformed pictures repreſented.

With reſpect to the latter, I wiſh we could gather from experience that the world was as readily laughed out of their follies as out of their goodneſs: I wiſh we had reaſon to be aſſured, that before any failure is drawn by ridicule from the breaſt, it is not neceſſary it ſhould be entirely out of faſhion.

Virtue being too much of this caſt is ſoon borne down, while folly, encircled with nu-

merous

merous advocates, is affected by fhame in the fame manner as Xerxes is reprefented to have been by the field of battle,—the laft in it, and the firft out of it.

A rigid honeft fatire has no quarter ; it is either thrown afide as a downright fcurrility, or only regarded from the exclufive merits of the diction. Add to this, that fcarce a character ventures to approve, the truths being fo feverely drawn, that delinquents (and how few are otherwife !) cannot bear to fee their own features fo roughly, and yet fo faithfully pourtrayed.

Thus the fpirit of acrimony too much affrights; that of ridicule too much diverts; and the fentiments not being polifhed into foftnefs, the fatirift is fcandalized as an officious, over-bearing cenfor, who prefumes to arraign the manners of others, before he has fufficiently examined whether his own are lefs reproachable.

Far

Far be it from me, however, to attempt the unreasonable vindication of a satiric dauber, who paints every feature, which his own affectation makes ungracious, beyond the life itself. Let such be loaded with that abuse which they impudently lavish on others, because their deserts are superior to their own. Yes, let the Censors, (like one of their brethren, who now prudently boasts his Northern extraction) be branded with perpetual infamy, while their malicious rancor turns satire into scandal, and truth into dishonest fiction, where truth only claims regard: doubly to be stigmatized, when they impiously vilify the very country to which they are a disgrace, by exaggerating, like a fashionable reflectory, her most attractive charms to a horrid and grotesque enormity.

Satiric mimicry, when exhibited in comedy, may sometimes be an exception to the foregoing assertion, having this superior advantage

advantage to the promotion of its fuccefs; the merits of the piece enforced by the qualities of the actor: In fatire merely narrative, the delineation of particular characters muft be circumftantially picturefque, or the defcription will neceffarily ftrike with fainter warmth, being refigned to the deliberate judgment of the reader, which in general may not be prefumed fufficient to keep pace with the fpirit of the performance; the comedian in the mean while fufpends the powers of reflection by his magic efficacy, and drawing into exiftence every feature, ftrikes you at once with the picture of the man he would reprefent.

Thus every fpark of humor and of acrimony leads a ready audience to the living character intended, and fo perfonally is the fatire applied, that no one is affronted by taking it for his own, except it be the real man, who gains not much by his know-

2   ledge,

ledge, having the powerful laugh of the world againſt him.

I ſhall not, after this premiſe, enter upon the worn-out compariſon between the merits of Juvenal and Horace, as ſa-tiric writers (Perſius, I think, is ſcarcely intitled to a place with them); I will con-ſider them only in one light, and leave the reader to judge of the propriety of my opinion.

It may be obſerved, that every tranſlator thinks himſelf bound to ſay ſomething in commendation of the author he attempts; but this rather, in truth, proceeds from a deſire of commending himſelf; as in ex-tolling the original he aſſumes a title to the ſame praiſes on his own (very often deficient) copy. Were he ſatisfied, how-ever, with this, the reader of a more for-giving temper might be inclined to excuſe

it,

it, as a vanity natural to an author. But the very next step he usually takes is to make invidious and self-sufficient comparisons between his author's manner, and that of others. As a far more distant copier I may be allowed to be a more distant commender; and have only to say, that in one respect I must esteem the conduct of Juvenal preferable to that of Horace.

Horace by his familiarity sometimes renders his poetry so extremely flat; it moves so very harsh and ungrateful to the ear, that we must confess it to be a degree worse than the stile "Sermoni propior." His sentiments simply dressed in prose would attract more than in that hobling verse which he adopts. Were it not for that singular delicacy, those polished strokes, with which his satire abounds, he might long ago have been laid aside, though now, in spite of his halting, admired by all.

Juvenal,

Juvenal, in the mean while, " Enfe
" velut ftricto," as he himfelf fays of Lu-
cilius, rufhes againft vice; he rarely flags
from that fire and fpirit which is as de-
lightfully ftriking to an Englifh ear as it
was fitted for a Roman's in thofe very degenerate times in which he wrote.

One fault indeed he, with the very beft
Roman authors, moft wildly runs into.
This is a fhamelefs and indifferent way of
conveying immodeft ideas. The natural
paffion ought always to be carefully rather
hinted than expreffed, that the innocent
may not be allured, nor the guilty diverted
from the moral propofed. This blemifh of
indelicacy Juvencius, in his edition of Juvenal, has been affiduous to remove; from
him therefore my imitations are framed :
that the omiffion of fuch reprefentations
may fhew the author in that high light
which his other fentiments demand.

A fecond

A fecond fault which he extravagantly purfues, is an exaggerated railing at women; it is a difagreeable, though a true remark, that many the moft engaging writers affect to form an indifferent opinion of the ladies; an error which from their example has corrupted thofe of lefs folid capacities, who glory in a dull cenfure of the fair, without being in reality any judges of their merit.

The fixth fatire is one repeated invective againft crimes which human nature, it may be prefumed, never was guilty of; but refentment, whether well or ill grounded, often calls upon the affiftance of fancy. So fevere did it appear even to Dryden, no great patron of the fex in general, that he efteemed himfelf under a neceffity to apologize for tranflating it: An apology which muft do him more honor with the civilized part of his readers, than he could

have

have defired from the moft faithful tranflation.

But the fame reafon which influenced
Dryden to undertake his tranflation, con-
ftrains me as particularly to imitate it.
The reader, however, will not be fur-
prized to find that I have varied many paf-
fages, that I have foftened exaggerations,
and not railed at guilt, which in my imitation could be but a creature of fancy;
and that I have only dwelt fometimes,
and that with reluctance, on the follies
which I have always thought to be but
fpecks on the fnowy minds of the fair.

As to my plan in general, I cannot fay
but that I met with many difficulties in
the execution of it: To fuit my characters
to thofe of Juvenal was not always eafy;
to fuit them in every article was impoffible.
That of Crifpinus in the fourth fatire is

cenfured

cenſured in ſuch outrageous colors, and
with ſuch a ſtudied aggravation, that an
example of blackneſs minutely coinciding
in the imitation, would have betrayed more
of private reſentment than of truth. La-
teranus's in the eighth is made up of ſuch
a variety of circumſtances, that I found
myſelf under a neceſſity to produce it into
two, and thoſe not very cloſe copies in
ſeveral paſſages. In the other parts of the
work I have endeavored to keep at as
convenient a diſtance as the nature of a
LIBERAL IMITATION would admit ; never
creeping ſtep by ſtep in a ſervil tranſlation,
nor altogether wantoning into the luxuriancy
of an original.

If I have been any where reduced to the
neceſſity of the latter, it will be chiefly ob-
ſervable in thoſe ſatires where I have varied
the original ſubject. The imitation of the
fourth, though generally adapted to my
author in the characters themſelves, is in-
trinſically

trinſically different as to the main deſign.
Whoever likewiſe examines into the general run of the ninth, will ſoon perceive
that the original is not, in many places,
cloſely copied. The candid reader may
however excuſe my having thereby ſoft-
ened the harſhneſs of vice, and made it, as
more generally now-a-days experienced,
the meer offspring of thoughtleſs folly.

As I am conſcious, on the whole, that I
have not cenſured without foundation, I
have not teſtified ſo ſcrupulous an humanity, as to heſitate cenſure where I had one;
and though I may be more forward to
commend virtue, I profeſs myſelf untinc-
tured with that faſtidious delicacy which
thinks that vice ought to be excuſed.

Severe repreſentations of high characters
may poſſibly give offence to ſome, ſome
whoſe more nice nature, like that of the ſen-
ſitive plant, ſhrinks at every touch of ſatire.

If

If I am freed, however, from the impu-
tation of injuftice, I fhall not only be able
to vindicate myfelf, but could, were my
abilities of a fuperior extent, prove fuch
cenfure to be requifite. The man of an
exalted fituation, if good, has a fuller title
to the refpect of mankind, by being placed
in a condition where his example may be
more inftrumental to infufe goodnefs into
others: But where he is bad, he calls forth
a double portion of condemnation, as his
depraved example may prove an epidemical
diftemper; may poifon every virtue, and
fow the rankeft feeds of vice and wicked-
nefs over the whole creation of human-
kind.

But if any thing might require a particular excufe, the drawing out SOME characters into light appears more immediately
to demand it: Characters, whofe PRIVATE
fituation may be efteemed a kind of veil
for their faults from the public eye, which

it is fcarcely honeſt to take off; but ſurely
this veil may as confiſtently be removed for
the diſplay of errors, as it would from
good nature be allowed to be for the diſplay of virtues. I know indeed that moſt
readers judge of the importance of the ſatire from the dignity of the ſubject; and
would eſteem the triumph of the pen over
INFERIOR delinquents in the ſame light as
they would that of Domitian over the
FLIES: dull entertainment for minds
whoſe only ambition it is to level every
one to their own infignificancy!

  That this is not entirely my ſentiment I
am proud to acknowledge; and have humility enough to think, that my muſe ſoars
not with that eagle flight that ſhe need be
aſhamed of ſtooping for her prey. Add to
this, that from the conduct of private characters a greater infight is in general had
into the GENUINE diſpofition, which in
thoſe of a public ſituation is ſo clouded
over

over by artificial circumftances, that you
feldom can know—the man.

From this confideration, the rude dif-
tichs on the humble tomb-ftone of a vil-
lager afford more fatisfactory entertainment
to the mind of the moralift, than the farce
and parade of coftly monuments in Weft-
minfter Abbey, erected too often by vanity
to gild the worft or meaneft characters.
Though a ramble in the latter regions may
be equally fitted for the meditation of the
fatirift, who may juftly efface the fuperfi-
cial infcriptions glaring on many of them,
and fix this HONEST epitaph:

Within thefe hallow'd realms th' ennobled dead,
Enfhrin'd in marble, rear their awful head;
Heroes, who perifh'd in the glorious ftrife;
Students, who calmly walk'd the vale of life;
Patriots, whofe torrent bad corruption fear;
And bards, whofe ftrains the virtuous deed revere:
To SUCH thefe lafting monuments are giv'n;
What THIS rewards, 'tis only known to Heav'n.

As

As to my author himself, though I think he carries throughout his performance an animated glow of thought, a rich masculine expression, I shall not undertake to assert that his severe arraignment of the vices of the age argues his own real probity of heart; a judgment which seems rather questionable from historical evidence; though Juvencius celebrates him in these words, " Fuisse probum ex eo appa-" ret, quo improbos ubiq; infectatur ar-" dore atq; impetu." If we look out into life we shall find the truth of this absolutely different; we shall find that the ablest lawyers, the most florishing statesmen, the most distinguished speakers, too often conform their actions very little to their words; and had Quintilian lived to this later season, he would by no means have had reason to assert, as he has done, that an able speaker MUST be an honest man.

[xxi]

As far as Juvenal's method has admitted
of it, I have endeavored to copy the manner of the admirable Young in his love of
fame. In Young we may obferve the elegant and delicate raillery of Horace, im-
proved by a happy verfification, and at the
fame time the fire and vehemence of Juvenal. In Pope, with all his fuperior fweetnefs of numbers, with all his beauty of
fentiments (which I would venture, even
in this age fo invidious of his memory, to
affert, are frequently original) I am con-
cerned to think, that the latter too much
predominates. In Swift we are repeatedly
ftruck with a coarfe wantonnefs of ill-na-
tured fatire, a peevifh morofenefs at the
creation of human-kind; which, though
painted in fuch colors that we cannot for-
bear laughter, the joke, I am afraid, upon
recollection turns ftrongly againft himfelf.
He feems, when fuch his mood, to be out
of temper with man, as if he grudged to
have been formed of the fpecies; or, as
the

the fagacious writer above-mentioned fays in his obfervations on Gulliver's Travels, (that proftitution of wit to burlefque humanity) " He has fo fatirized human na-
" ture as to give a demonftration in him-
" felf, that it deferves to be fatirized *."

Such a track my inclination leads me not implicitly to follow ; though I highly efteem his fpirit, when exercifed to degrade corruption, I am not fo frantic a mifanthrope as to take a pleafure, becaufe of the follies and vices, in throwing a flur upon the virtues of the world.

> " Curfe on the ftrain, how well foe'er it flow,
> " That tends to make one worthy man my foe."
>
> POPE.

I fhall conclude the Preface without offering the SLIGHTEST apology to the judgment of thofe who, I am aware, will ef-

* Conjectures on Original Compofition.

teem

teem this an unpromifing undertaking,
after that tranflation of my author's fatires
to which the name of Dryden is prefixed.
I readily acknowledge, that thofe executed
by that great mafter of numbers poffefs a
fingular degree of merit; but it may rea-
fonably be queftioned, whether his affift-
ants have fo happily fucceeded. A curfory
comparifon of his tranflations with thofe
of his brethren (who feem placed in the
edition as foils to him) will juftify the ap-
prehenfion; unlefs we except that elegant
verfion of the thirteenth fatire by Mr.
Creech, which fhines (fo admirably can a
poet fometimes rife above himfelf) equal,
if not fuperior, to the beft.

Let THESE, however, thus taught to be
extravagant admirers of our predeceffors,
reflect, that there is a material difference
between a TRANSLATION and an IMITA-
TION; fo material that they admit not of
comparifon; and then let them affume
their

their natural right of judging for themfelves, and not fleep contentedly over a
crude notion eftablifhed by other capacities,
equally infufficient with their own.

Upon the whole, my endeavors are
here exerted to prefent the public with a
juft comparifon between the MANNERS of
my author's, and thofe of our own times;
and if my readers are in general fo indulgent as to fmile upon a ftrain that means
but to be HONEST, I fhall efteem my labors amply rewarded, happy in being ca-
pable of adminiftring to their entertainment by an imitation of the SPIRITED
JUVENAL.

THE

SATIRES

OF

JUVENAL

IMITATED.

THE

FIRST SATIRE

IMITATED.

AUTHORS, be gone; enthufiaft tribe, away;
Clofe the trite page, nor trill the flimfy lay:
Shall felf-puft'd Brown eternal triumphs hope,
Jingling fatiric elegies on Pope?
With epithetic ftrut fhall facred rage
Ape the full majefty of Dryden's page?
In mimic plumes defcriptive weaknefs trick,
And make, by curing Saul, the reader fick?
Shall Honor grace the thoughts, and not the man? *
Hence, let all fuch go ruft with Athelftan.
See, the gay Cenfor's felf-reforming rage
Sullies the fplendors of his former page

---

* See Dodfley's Collection of Poems, vol. iii.

(Whofe

(Whofe gentle whet a † banquet huge proclaims,
With all the ‡ lawn-fleev'd goffip's fleepy flames)
Where thinly-fcatter'd letters fcarcely hide,
Or, patch-like, fairer fhew the paper's fnowy pride

In ftrains congenial venal Pamphleteers
Show'r forth their witlefs fcandal to the ears ;
Still fpringing fiercer from the flames of war,
Thefe infects blaft the foldier, and the tar ;
To cenfure blown by fafhion's giddy breath
They teize the hero, and the world to death.
The monthly upftarts ftill from merit tear
The bays, themfelves can never hope to wear ;
Forc'd to unwilling fmiles their ranc'rous breaft
Soils worth fuperior with a pointlefs jeft :
I fee not for applaufe ; let dullnefs raife
The kindred hirelings with the roar of praife.

Infpir'd by fuch I ftrike with cenfuring plan
The erring author, and the guilty man ;
Tho' the hand falters with the fears of youth,
I rufh indignant in the caufe of truth ;
Start, confcious guilt ! and blufh, prefumptuous pride !
No fhade fhall veil you, and no corner hide.

† See the advertifing puff prefixed.
‡ Burnet. See Swift, vol. viii. art. 4. fmall edit.

Come

Come then, O Satire, roam th' extended town
With fmile farcaftic, and the low'ring frown;
But ftill the patron of the virtuous train
Bid honeft juftice check th' impetuous rein.

Degen'rate times! what torment to behold
Unnumber'd votaries to the fhrine of gold!
What dregs of earth! what refufe of the land!
Who fcarce of old one vaffal could command,
Who crofs'd to Britain's fhore the boift'rous feas,
World-wand'ring Jews, and fawning Refugees,
Now ftalking high in fortune's profp'rous hour
Load wealth on wealth, and wriggle into pow'r.
See fondly melting at the fummer's heat,
Sighing they fink into the fhade's retreat!
True men of tafte the fhrubb'ry's walks prepare,
Then curfe the clime, that made them what they are.
See from their chariots to the crowd below,
To nobles felves th' exalted mifcreants bow;
Ev'n yields my Lady's heart to wealth the ftrife,
And pays due rev'rence to the Tradefman's wife.

Yon foul, my mufe, to confcious light difplay,
Flufh'd with the treafures of a nation's pay;
Yet ev'n the ftate, infatiate of the ftore,
Which from the dunghill rais'd him, cheats for more.
Difhoneft wretch! let fatire make thee pine,
Nor leave thee punifh'd with a trifling Fine;

Leave

Leave thee no more, vain Dotard, in thy age
The Park to wander, or at cards to rage.

Let other's praifes Shandy's page proclaim,
Which thro' wit's labyrinth rambles into fame;
Let flutt'ring youth, on Novel's reftlefs wing,
To grafps of vifionary tranfports fpring:
Satire, I all am thine; no fofter lure
My ftrains fhall lull, no myft'ry fhall obfcure.

View the rich Trifler of Newmarket's plain,
Who fhines chief jockey mid the juggling train,
Now martial burn in glory's fcenes reveal'd,
And feek the triumphs of a diff'rent field;
A well-drefs'd foldier ftrut before his band,
And for a feafon quit the turf's command.

Hark! at each footftep reafon's voice I find,
" Go, take the pen, and fatirize thy kind;"
Draw forth the delicate, fantaftic man,
Coop'd up, and powder'd in the clofe fedan;
Strip the gay plumage to the noon-tide air,
And blaft this lifping mimic of the fair;
This minion, who immers'd in folly's toys
The wealth of violated trufts enjoys.
Draw forth the bride, to footh the fick man's foul
Whofe impious hands prepar'd the pois'nous bowl;

Then

Then bore defpondent forrow's fable veft ·
To footh the flanders of the world to reft.

Dare nobly, man, nor fortune's fmile fhall fail,
Crimes worthy well the gibbet, and the jail;
Prefumptuous vice repeated glories raife,
While needy virtue meets but empty praife.
The manfion's pride, th' attendants and the plate,
The fmoaking board, the vanities of ftate,
Shine forth for vice; for vice, tho' fir'd by zeal,
Which modeft virtue blufhes to reveal:
Glow, glow, my mufe, th' enflaming theme to fit,
That Lockman's felf would kindle into wit.

Ere fince the ark, high-tow'ring o'er the wave,
Defy'd the guilty world's furrounding grave,
And new-born earth recruited ftrength improv'd,
Which heav'n re-peopled by the man it lov'd,
The fond defires, the giddy cares of life,
The bufy tranfports, and the wayward ftrife,
The rambling paffions human fouls difplay,
All, all, I fnatch them to the face of day.

Vice proudly ftalks triumphant o'er the field,
And bids at once dejected virtue yield;
She decks with two-fold charms the founding die,
By her fell avarice lures the dazzled eye;

By

By her vain fashion, wrapp'd in gay delight,
Spends with a wretch a fortune in a night;
False honor's loffes load the future day;
For honor's debts no peers refuse to pay.

See, to a villain's use the treasures roll,
Meant for a bleffing to their owners' foul;
To patience forc'd each insolence they view,
No gold referv'd supplies the vaffal's due.
Now flowly opes the late-refounding gate,
Few mourn dejected grandeur's fhatter'd ftate;
If e'er the footftep of some pitying friend,
Some forrowing heart, the well-known dome attend,
Each fhudd'ring look the horrid bailiff fhews,
A dun he hears in ev'ry gale that blows;
And juft his care; for with a knelling roar
Thefe ghaftly fons of evil crowd the door;
A ftern, curs'd train, the conquerors of play,
Croak round like ravens, till they're gorg'd with pay.

Meanwhile the wealthy Cit with haughty air
Pours the rude censure on afflictive care;
" See there the fool, th' uwieldy upftart cries;
" There, prefs'd with want, the man of fashion lies;
" 'Twas thine in toys, in trifles to efface
" The wealth and fplendor of thy boafted race;
" Life's murder'd hours with gilded knaves to lead,
" Till folly funk thee to the vale of need.

" Be

" Be Mine by prudence to enhance my fame,
" And rear o'er fons of gold my deathlefs name;
" From trade, ye great, my treafur'd joys I bring,
" Nor grudge, tho' riches from a counter fpring."

Thus, wealth, thus ftill thy head o'er title rear,
Flufh'd from the witchcraft of a South-Sea year;
Thou, genial wealth, whofe charms refiftlefs glow,
The firft divinity of man below :
No priefts, 'tis true, thy imag'd idol greet
With meek devotion proftrate at thy feet ;
In vows no Chriftians at thine altar bend,
Nor call thee, gold, their father and their friend ;
Yet afk the heart, thy boundlefs fway to prove,
What heart but views thee with a look of love !

Survey the fair, when winter's frowns begin,
And mark their follies, for they know no fin ;
Each ev'ning's vifits an unnumber'd heap,
They prize th' acquaintance from the flaves they keep;
The flaves, who gayly dancing round the board
To tradefmen vend the cuftom of their lord.
Coop'd in the filken confines of a chair,
Now iffues to her Friends the thoughtlefs fair ;
While my lord's jumbled in his coach alone
(The pair by fafhion feparately fhewn)
Or, if abhorrent of the tirefome rout,
Bids Madam leave his ticket, where they're out.

For

For ever idle, and yet ne'er at reſt,
Thus roams in giddy toils the female breaſt;
Her only care, the hurrying flutter paſs'd,
She muſt, muſt wander to her Spouſe at laſt.

What frolic whims the varying great control!
What rambling fancies captivate his foul'!
While morning ſleep ſtill lingers on his eyes,
Some-where to hide him from himſelf he flies;
Saunters to ſhops, the coffee-houſe, and law,
Next modiſh artiſts his attention draw,
Where taſte may many an aukward piece proclaim,
Whoſe daubing frowns diſgraceful of the frame.
Then roams the ſick'ning rambler to the Park,
And meets ſome idle, thoughtleſs brother-ſpark;
Shakeſpear's the word; he hurries on before,
And fixes dinner—ſomething after four.
Fantaſtic ſlaves! can pleaſures flow ſincere,
Where Want of happineſs is bought ſo dear?

Behold the buſy peer, whoſe reſtleſs eye
Exhauſts for prey the regions of the ſky;
Toils o'er the main, o'er earth's remoteſt ſeat,
To deck the pride of an election-treat;
Whoſe coſtly board ſuch ſumptuous treaſure fills,
'Twould coſt a fortune—did he pay the bills.
How will your pity riſe enflam'd to hate,
When ſuch the bulwark of a ſinking ſtate!

See,

See, what defpondence damps his forrowing breaft,
While ftripp'd of dear-lov'd grandeur's fplendid veft!
Still fadly penfive wears the lonely hour,
Till confcious tranfport fpeaks returning pow'r;
Ev'n then the ftatefman evil's frown attends,
Spurn'd by his foes, lamented by his friends.

Hail, heart-fteel'd heroes of thefe worthlefs days,
Whofe life one complicated guilt difplays!
Whofe fhamelefs deeds abafh'd the filial train
Will pant and toil to emulate in vain;
With fighing bofom quit th' unequal chace,
And curfe the footfteps, which they cannot trace!
For you bold fatire fpreads her daring wings,
On the full breeze with rapid ardor fprings:
O for the genius of thofe halcyon times,
When honeft freedom could proclaim the crimes,
Stem'd the wild torrent of a guilty town,
Nor fear'd the vengeance of a ftatefman's frown!

Hint but in fatire's ftrain th' exalted Peer,
Alas! the pillory and the jail appear!
Blefs'd if Sh—b—r's thy mitigated fate,
Tho' truth direct the venom of thy hate;
That hate of former fchemes, whofe rage demands
The fatt'ning penfion from the Northern's hands.
Heed then the ribband's pride, the fplendid ftar;
Pay awful rev'rence to the gilded car;

5

Nor

Nor dare diſplay him, tho' his crimes are ſet
More ſtrong to ſtamp him than his coronet.

Let Epic Glover tune the lofty ſtrain
To heroes worthy of an Engliſh reign,
Who glow with free-born dignity, nor ſpeak
Like * Wilkie's, ev'ry ſentence from the Greek:
Let the mild Bard ſtill court th' elegiac page,
Too peaceful for the ode's enthuſiaſt rage:
When Pope, forth iſſuing with reſiſtleſs force,
'Gainſt hell-born falſhood bends his eager courſe,
How ſhrink, with guilt appall'd, the ſlaves of ſin,
And tremble, conſcious of the crime within!
Swift-ruſhing tears the deep-felt pangs proclaim,
Which curſe the ſatire, that they dare not blame.
And yet theſe daſtard ſouls, whoſe boaſted might
Retires unequal to the deſp'rate fight,
The vengeful ſtreams on ſlumb'ring genius ſhed,
And whom they living fear'd, arraign when dead.

* The Epigoniad.

THE

THE

SECOND SATIRE

IMITATED.

LONDON, farewel; far from thy bounds I roam
To fome Utopia's hofpitable home;
Far hence, where man, the creature of deceit,
In looks an Allen, is in heart a cheat.

Here learning's votaries, with repeated toil
Who wafte the thoughtful hour, and midnight oil,
Deck'd with all Athens' ftores, are fcarcely known,
Unlefs fome upftart name the papers crown;
While falfe pretenders, whofe refplendent cafe
Perhaps a Shakefpear, or a Milton grace,
Beam with the fire of each poetic thought,
Their Inkhorn's felf with erudition fraught.

Lo!

Lo! filently demure they ftalk along,
The vacant mimics of the wifer throng;
More honeft far the lean, diftemper'd peer,
Stamp'd on whofe frame the flagrant faults appear;
Whofe falt'ring ftep, and fhrivel'd face difplay
The full debauch'ries of his younger day.

Hence, Cromwells, hence, who founds of peace impart,
The dagger lifted at your country's heart;
Who 'gainft adult'ry wage a gen'rous ftrife,
Warm from th' embraces of their neighbour's wife:
The flaves of ftate, who damn the venal tribe,
With hand ftill open for the welcome bribe;
I hate them all; who rage of zeal employ,
Betray the Jefuit, lurking to deftroy.
Yes, when I view the ftern fevere grimace,
I know hypocrify's delufive face;
Pitt's thoughts the virtuous talker fhould control,
And bellowing generals prove a Marlborough's foul.

Proud of the facred pulpit's lov'd renown
The cloifter'd ftripling hurries to the gown;
" Why flumbers worth," he cries, with fhame o'erfpread,
" While vice licentious rears her daring head?"
Aufpicious days! a greater Whitfield rife,
And point the dæmons frowning to our eyes. *

* See Mr. Hogarth's print alluded to SAT. VI.

Alas!

Alas! the zealot ſcan; you'll find the ſcarf,
The gloves, and kerchief are the better half;
While he, from ſallies of fermenting blood,
Roars a fit member of the Robin-Hood.

Yet, ſtripling, ceaſe; for vain thy watchful care;
Go, leave the burden to ſome ſhallow mayor;
His be the taſk of vagrants, whoſe pretence
From pomp of pray'r to ſin without offence;
Such from oppoſing doctrine firmer ſtand,
And blaſt with indolence devotion's land.
Thy ſpotleſs ſoul, if virtuous actions grace,
Go, ſpurn corrupted conduct to the face;
Spurn ev'n the man, whom menial ſins delight,
Expert in law, yet ſtranger to the right;
Full on the fair whoſe eyes for ever rove,
A new Alcides in the cauſe of love;
He holds the diſtaff with the ſofteſt grace,
And ſpins more ſubt'ly than Arachne's race:
Such livelier fancies Claudius' ſoul tranſport;
He flies for bliſs the dullneſs of a court.
Alas! with partial venom cenſure flows,
We doves are ſtain'd, tho' faultleſs ſtrut the crows;
Elſe unreprov'd had Claudius' vagrant heart
Sunk to the baſeneſs of debauch'ry's art,
Sunk manhood's glory in the mire of ſin,
The judge without, the proſtitute within.

Say,

Say, lovely nymph, whofe parents' ftricter plan
Will fcarce admit thee ev'n a look at man,
Why thofe fantaftic whims, thofe airy arts,
With folly's baits to catch at human hearts?
'Tis fafhion, ruling fafhion, draws thee in;
That fiend, fo often made a plea for fin.
To this alike the prince and peafant yield;
Maids at the toilette; heroes in the field:
She rules the lawyer's and phyfician's toil,
And fattens Scotland on an Englifh foil;
Thence many a fcheming, plodding tool of late
Glides into court, and balances the ftate.

Yet love of fafhion fits the female breaft;
Not fo the zeal to blaft another's reft,
Which to coarfe cenfure fires the prieftly heart,
The meagre flave of delicacy's art;
Shaking with ev'ry gale, whofe fondling care
Condemns the infant to the healthy air:
Shall such enhance with aggravated hate,
The fancy'd mis'ries of a gen'rous ftate,
And urge the crew of fcriblers to withftand,
Like him, the ftrong contagion of the land?
Like him, true fons of licence to advance,
And waft each virtue of the foil to France?
Ill-fated wretch! whom manly dictates warm,
To fink to foft effeminacy's charm!

To

To fink bemir'd in felf-conviction's way,
And blaſt with eſtimating ſpite * th' Eſſay :
There, there alone, thy triumphs feaſt the ſight,
Where the pen vibrates in the cauſe of right.

Mark but fantaſtic pleaſure's frolic train,
What giddy vot'ries croud her ſplendid reign !
See, to the flow'ry throne their ſteps advance,
Inſpir'd to love, to muſic, and the dance :
At pleaſure's fane aſſemble EV'N the fair ;
The mode how diff'rent for the houſe of pray'r !
Here Florio ſhines, in ſilken charms array'd,
And boaſts thoſe conqueſts which he never made.
Such beauty fills his mien, ſuch fire his eyes,
Each maid for Florio pines, for Florio dies.
With rougher voice, leſs poliſh'd Ebrius roars,
Fluſh'd from the rude embrace, and Bacchus' ſtores ;
Bellows the conqueſts of the verdant courſe,
And loves far leſs his miſtreſs than his horſe ;
At friends he ſwears when adverſe runs oppreſs,
And damns himſelf, 'cauſe fortune grudg'd ſucceſs.

The ſob'rer Stateſman, who with ruling hand
Controls the houſe, and clamors thro' the land,
The ruder paſſions damp'd by cooler years,
From court the lord's reſplendent title bears ;

* Eſſay on Characteriſtics.

C   Fluſh'd

Flufh'd with whofe fweets the thunders roll no more,
And mildnefs charms the friend, the foe before.
Was it for this, in richeft glory great,
Thou pour'dft the torrent on the Slave of ftate?
Was it for this, at oppofition's call,
Thy fury drove corruption to the wall?
To difappointed man the truth to own,
That Cotta's patriot for himfelf alone.

Survey the glow of grandeur's coftly board:
What fhamelefs converfe courts the prattling Lord!
While healthlefs claret fires his modifh vein,
He lifps indecency's ill-manner'd ftrain;
Or the full glafs the brutal roarings crown,
That toafts the reigning miftrefs of the town;
While ftanzas coarfe fly iffuing from his tongue,
Which his felf-flatt'ring frenzy terms a fong.
Indulgent Heav'n! fome rigid Cato fend,
Some virtuous cenfor, virtue to defend;
Strike upftart error from our guilty plan,
And make each vice a prodigy in man.

Let Railers baul, that England's fons of old
Difplay'd the hero, gen'rous, rough, and bold:
That now in tinfel joys they wafte their bloom,
Soft in attire, and fcented with perfume;
Low funk the flumb'ring foul, life's worthlefs care,
The news, the park, the tavern, and the play'r:
I call

I call ye not, ye fhades, immortal hoft,
Once the brave champions of my native coaft,
To view with confcious grief the fcene of woe,
The hero fall'n a fribble and a beau.

No—the great bofom's kindling flame difplays
The FULL-BLOWN glories of our ancient days;
Undaunted Granby quits his native fhore,
Proud of th' embattled field, and cannon's roar;
See gen'rous Clive, undazzled by a throne,
To fcepter'd boldnefs hafte the parting groan:
O'er Land, o'er Ocean, fwells th'expanded fire,
Where Pocock's laurel'd deeds to fame infpire;
Where Hawke, untainted by corruption, fprings,
Whofe merit, crufh'd by Statefmen, fhone to kings:
Blufh, blufh, ye daftards, to behold the toil,
Ye backward fouls, ye S———s of our ifle.

No Chriftian Prieft with falfe religion's fhow'rs
Celeftial Oil o'er meek repentance pours;
Nor rigid fiend th' unmeaning whip prepares,
When imag'd Mary fpurns his eager pray'rs;
Yet reafon's voice exclaims, 'mid worldly ftrife,
The foul glows confcious of another life.
Had humble Bradford elfe, for virtue's fake,
Felt the dire horrors of the wheel and ftake?
Had Cranmer, dauntlefs at impending death,
Flam'd the mean hand, which fought protracted breath?

C 2

They, rob'd in blifs, exalted in the fky,
Survey degen'rate man with pitying eye ;
And wifh, difcumber'd from his earthly clay,
His foul unfpotted fhone as pure as they.

Hail, England, hail! I hear with joy refound
Thy martial deeds o'er earth's extended round :
O'er Gallia's coafts thy dread alarms have fhow'r'd,
And ev'n on India's realms their terrors pour'd.
Yet, yet, beware; let Sin's alluring art
No longer fix it's empire o'er thy heart ;
Heav'n's injur'd arm at length may ftrike the blow,
And thofe, who fpurn'd the friend, lament the foe.

THE

THE

THIRD SATIRE

IMITATED.

WHILE confcious forrow, ftill a foe to art,
    With cloifter'd ———'s abfence fills my heart;
    Fair friendfhip's ftrains muft hail the deftin'd
        fpot,
Where, fince his fall, Newcaftle is forgot.
Methinks once more Cam's muddy banks I rove,
Or fmile amid the gloom of Margaret's grove;
For there, fecure from London's curs'd alarm,
Rook'ries muft chear me, folitude muft charm:
There, plung'd in books, no Party-flames you dread,
Nor mourn, tho' Benet totter round your head;
Tho' high o'er genius pedant labors rife,
And Scott ftill walks the courfe for Seaton's prize.

To learning's ancient realm I fpeed my way,
But fix on London's verge a tranfient ftay;
Hard by the fane, where Whitfield's holy guefts
Throw in their pence, and ply their am'rous feafts;
Tho' foon their chief may mourn the beggar'd fpot,
So wooes our ftrong idolatry the Scot:
The Scot, whom fondly church, and S——e behold,
And crown with worth, with genius, and with Gold.

Fir'd at the flaves of fraud I eye the coaft,
Where ftalks forth violated reafon's ghoft;
Where to deluded fouls the prieftly Fool
Roars floods of folly with RAPACIOUS rule;
Whofe full trimm'd phrafe ne'er deviates into Senfe,
And truth is loft in matchlefs impudence.

When thus, indignant of the fhamelefs town,
I paufe, and fpurn it with contemptuous frown;
Since then diffus'd o'er guilt's detefted foul
Wealth, grandeur, ftreaming in full triumph roll;
Since honeft toil infures a poor regard,
And baffled virtue droops without reward;
Since wafteful hours my little all confume;
Ere want's difgraceful horrors ftamp my doom,
While pants my bofom with the love of truth,
And fav'ring confcience confecrates my youth,
Carelefs of grandeur, to the world unknown,
My will fupported by myfelf alone,

I quit

I quit the stage, nor quit it with chagrin,
When herds of letter'd hirelings croud the scene:
Creatures whose souls corrupted passions move,
Who damn the treasure, that at heart they love;
Who cringe to ministers, but curse the great,
And, spurning minions, are the tools of state;
By party dup'd deny with faithless Pride
Their friend, as Peter once his Lord deny'd;
Rank Tories, who with smiles a court behold,
And sell their country for their country's gold.

Such, such, of old the tongues of foul abuse,
To patrons, proudly they disown'd, of use;
Whose strains, when passion swell'd the kindred ire,
With factious venom fann'd the streaming fire,
Such, flush'd with triumph, and sworn idols grown,
Low'r stern defiance on the nation's frown:
So rudely jesting Chance the die has cast,
" The last we find the first, the first the last."

But say, can London's scenes my fondness meet?
Falshood with friendly smile I cannot greet;
I cannot view Fingal with ravish'd eye,
That English, Galic, High-Dutch rhapsody;
I cannot DOOM the sire to please the heir,
——Your task, ye sons of second-sighted care;
To gull the Virgin I no gifts impart,
Nor drawl out love, with mischief in my heart;

C 4

No

No fraud, like knighted Juſtice, can I ſmother,
Or ſet one deſp'rate Rogue to catch another;
Vice, whatſoe'er her ſhape, I dare deteſt,
But chiefly ſpurn her in a princely breaſt:
Thus live I now, and thus I ſeek my end,
No puff my virtue, and no wretch my friend.

    But what is friendſhip? is the bleſſing dear?
Our Friends by ſin are made, confirm'd by fear;
The guilty ſecret fondly I impart,
The ſecret for a vent which rends HIS heart;
Thence, fix'd by prudence, cannot force its way,
Becauſe in turn this friend I can betray.

    What crouded crimes impartial eyes behold!
Crimes to fair innocence, transform'd by gold;
But thou, ſhould England's laviſh treaſures roll
Laviſh as thoſe, which fed the German ſoul,
Or thoſe whoſe ſplendors far more laviſh feed
The ten-toe couriers from the banks of Tweed;
Guilt's tools diſdain, and hug thy happier ſtate,
No darling eye-ſore of the jealous great.

    Point, unrelenting ſatire, point the herd,
Slaves of the great, and by the great preferr'd;
Yes, tear them forth; unmov'd I cannot ſee
Poor England ſink a Scotiſh colony:

Ill-fated

Ill-fated England! foe to wifdom's call!
The fport of nations, with the dregs of all!
Dupe to the bugbears of the Spaniard's pride!
By wafte and luxury to France ally'd!
Inftructed by our foes to curfe the war,
We dance, lifp French, and jingle the guittar.

How mourn the laurels, blafted in their bloom!
How vanquifh'd kingdoms fmile o'er England's doom!
Whofe head degraded droops with modifh hate;
—This comes of raifing Scotfmen to the f——e.

Creatures, ne'er feen before, St. J——s's greet,
Profcribing ev'ry Englifhman they meet;
Names far too great for barb'rous Englifh verfe,
And only fit to ftrut in genuine Erfe.
Form'd for deceit, the fettled front furvey,
Genius, thro' ev'ry toil that ftems her way:
Hark! from their throats what whining periods croak!
Periods, which ne'er like England's, end in fmoke.

Yet not unjuftly Scotland lures our hearts;
She brings a world of fciences and arts.
Can books unread, and men unknown, abufe,
And eke out novels, magazines, Reviews.
With conjurers of all forts feafts the fight:
Her Priefts in bufkins trip, her Lairds can write;

Hift'ry

Hiſt'ry complete ſhe ſends in Smollet's name;
Epic on Epic ſwells Macpherſon's fame;
Maul-it with meek preſumption dares to own
Bute barely ſecond to the king alone.
THERE each mechanic ſoars on learning's wings,
And thoſe, who work for bread, are ſprung from kings;
Kings all themſelves, they beg with haughty eye,
And curſe the hand, that gives them charity.

Shall ſuch in ſofteſt ſilks beſiege the great,
Theſe aukward Novices to lux'ry's ſtate?
Such riſe our lords in Deed, as well as Thought?
Such who more Plagues than One to England brought.

Is it for this we boaſt our fertil plains,
The ſoil where glory ſoars, and freedom reigns?
While dwindles to a Scot the doting mind,
Curs'd with an Union Nature ne'er deſign'd.
Still ſhall we liſten to their treach'rous call?
Still ſhall we hug the race which hates us all?
Shall, harden'd as their hearts, their members claim
The manly roughneſs of the Britiſh frame?
Hence with the ſtrain of fulſome flattery;
Hence from your idols learn the art to lie.

Around, their triumphs ſwell; the partial ſtage
Puffs MODEST Merit to the taſteful age:

There

There flimfy Aquileïa drawls for praife ;
There Agis all his Nothingnefs difplays ;
Bute's * peaceful puffer there Elvira fhines,
And breaks off in a huff her lazy lines ;
Hail, Garrick, hail, whofe pow'rs unbounded ftream,
Can conjure meaning from a vacant theme !

Mark the fond friends ; you cannot laugh or cry
But thefe deluders bear you company ;
Is there an oddity provokes your mirth ?
They'll fwear you are the wittieft foul on earth:
Yet heed their treach'ry ; for at diftance due
They'll get fome other friend, and laugh at you.
No match for fuch, I ween, the Englifh heart,
Who borrow looks to fhine in any part :
Their happy mufcles to their heart a fcreen,
No Conjurer can tell you what they mean :
Thus arm'd, your houfe they haunt, your fecrets hear,
Difguis'd to mar your peace, and make you fear.

Full-harden'd into pride by rugged rules,
Tofs'd to the world from ftiff pedantic fchools,
The ftores of learning op'd to THEM alone,
They ftrut, and damn all knowledge, but their own ;
Then fwear from Scotland letters firft began,
And the firft rays of fcience beam'd on man.

* See the dedication, which flows with all the Spirit of the tragedy.

Crown,

Crown, wealth and grandeur, crown the fons of Art,
Who bear no Stranger near a Patron's heart;
Our treafures ravifh'd by their fpecial grace,
WE 're hurry'd out, and THEY ufurp our place;
With poifon fraught the filken dictates roll,
Play round the head, and fteal into the foul;
Blown by THEIR baleful breath the ftorm defcends,
And low'rs on All, that dare be England's Friends.

See what thick fquadrons crowd to Galba's door,
Squadrons of meanly great, and richly poor;
Flutt'ring in bufy idlenefs the while
They ken the MON who wins the foft'ring fmile;
For ever bafking in the blazing ray
From a thick cloud juft rifen into day.
THERE England's Relics grin with fimp'ring grace;
There frown the horrors of the Northern face;
There the fpruce Stripling ftudies Statefmen's tricks;
There Prebends pant to loll in Bifhoprics;
There Warriors ftand rich Regiments to feize;
And Pleafure's fons grow fat with Agencies.

Mark the convincing proof of B———d's wit,
That dares to brand the poverty of P———;
Who fiercely rufhing on the fons of pride,
Adher'd to meafures which he could not GUIDE.
Tho' thoufand minions on THEIR lux'ry wait,
Tho' land on land proclaim THEIR vaft eftate;

Tho'

Tho' France for THEM her richeſt feaſts employ,
As here our courtiers welcome Nivernois;
I cannot deem, among the ſons of earth,
That wealth and grandeur are the road to Worth.
No, heav'n-born Juſtice, THY award will clear
With ſmiles alike, the Poor-man, or the Peer;
On this in vain the ſolemn Oath is paſs'd,
And Honor's Word comes uſeleſs from the laſt.

What tho' the PLAIDED RUG's coarſe tatter'd veſt
Provoke in Engliſh ſouls th' eternal jeſt;
Tho' the flat Bonnet's niggard round is ſpread,
As jocularly meant to mock the head;
Which points a wretch to Famine near ally'd,
Spite of the pompous Sword, that loads his ſide;
(So their faſt friends the French immers'd in dirt
The rich-work'd Ruffle boaſt, without the Shirt)
Tho' ridicule contemn the ſordid Elves,
The ſtream, alas! is turn'd againſt Ourſelves.

" Hence, England, hence, ill-ſuited to the Great;
" 'Tis Ours to riot in the chair of ſtate;
" To fatten on the land, where Plenty reigns,
" The tools to ev'ry taſk, that B—— ordains;
" Each Scotiſh Laird ſhall quit his MENIAL trade,
" And ſhine ſupreme in ſplendid Robes diſplay'd;
" Each beggar here to cloſe his cares ſhall ſpeed
" By England's goodneſs beckon'd from the Tweed.

" Your

" Your Daughters honor'd with a Scotfman's arms
" Shall freely give their Treafures, and their charms;
" No fordid Famine fhall difgrace our heirs;
" Their heads fhall regulate the kingdom's cares;
" In wealth and grandeur they fecure fhall reign,
" Without a thought of vent'ring back again."

By virtue's aid the Scot difdains to rife;
Deceit performs the tafk in wifdom's guife;
Strong is HIS heart in fraud, as England's weak;
OUR wealth they want, WE give them what they feek,
Our honeft fouls on Scripture-plan proceed;
We " clothe the naked, and the hungry feed;"
Subftantial banquets glut thefe fons of Eafe,
Their native Oatmeal can no longer pleafe;
Crown'd with their fmiles the Plaid and Bonnet thrive,
By England vainly quafh'd in—Forty-five.

SUCH ftrut, from felf-conceit the firft of earth,
Tho' fhiv'ring bare-foot from their earlieft birth;
Around whofe coafts no verdure cheers the eye,
Blefs'd with no flighteft Glimpfe of jollity;
Unlefs when aping human founds they bawl
" Some bo-nie A-pifode fra' fene Fingal;"
While gazing on his Jaw's diftended charms
Each Mother clafps her Warbler in her arms.

No

No Changeling mode of drefs difplays the man,
True honor dignifies each fteady Clan;
Bafe wealth's corrupting Glow is THERE unknown;
And lux'ry centers in the Plaid alone.
While England, paltry upftart of the earth,
Leaps nature's bounds, and clothes—beyond her worth;
Unlefs from int'reft WE fcarce own a brother,
And, when in want, we pilfer from each other;
Tho' rough, luxurious, drunken with our ftore,
To ev'ry Fool that knocks we ope our door;
Our fupple hearts to EV'RY fafhion fuit,
And our own PITT forfake to worfhip B———.

Curs'd with expences ev'n to Friends we roam,
Each private manfion is corruption's dome:
How would our fathers' honeft anger glow
To fee the livery'd Minions in a row!
While from my friend the long-known welcome fails,
When once I DARE neglect his Servants' vails.

Who fear'd of old the country's mild retreat?
No ruin hover'd o'er the peaceful feat;
Thofe fcenes a tranfient refpite could difpenfe
From wafte of cares, from riot, and expence.
In thefe ftrange times, when changes tofs the great,
And fcarce a thread fupports the man of ftate;
Tho' prudent B——e has bid the Battle ceafe,
And England, murm'ring, eyes her fcars in peace,

Taxes

Taxes on taxes heap'd the foul affright :
What wonder Lux'ry still usurps the Light !
The Light, so deeply tax'd, by Nature free :
Plain proof that all things to our cost we see !
Nay, burdens pil'd on burdens load the Day :
Excise for food, for drink, for life we pay.
Houses a cumbrance to their owners stand,
Mortgag'd for PUBLIC debts, as well as land :
While PRIVATE mortgage swells the wasteful fire,
And rears the mountain of OUR OWN the higher.
Thrice happy ye, whom Nature's self denies
To furnish England's wants with GREAT supplies.

What if in Scotland's wilds we veil'd our head,
Where tempests whistle round the sordid bed ;
Where the Rug's two-fold use we might display,
By night a blanket, and a plaid by day ;
Where ever-lasting Sands fatigue the eye,
B—e's high-daub'd form to feast our loyalty ;
Books ere the deluge scrawl'd, our taste to call,
Such as the learn'd Macpherson swears Fingal :
Bless'd with these little Perquisites alone,
We still shall call those Perquisites our own ;
Free-Masons all, no want shall starve our Clan,
Where each assists his Brother, ALL HE CAN ;
Where careless we may sneer at England's curse,
While her own treasures fill our scanty purse.

Truc

True Scots transform'd, for us their p—rs shall fall,
For us their chiefs shall fight, their m——rs bawl;
Their priests, as usual, 'gainst their country move,
And doat on Scotsmen with a Scotsman's love.
Ev'n now I see the welcom'd period rise;
Our chariots roll, our structures mate the skies;
For us the painter's art on Scotland's shore
Shall dress the Landscape's form, unknown before;
For us the Statue's animated grace
Shall swell the earlier Patriarchs of our race;
At college only Jamie shall not bloom,
Drawn at full length to glare in ev'ry room.
Thus fatt'ning plenty shall rejoice our race,
Health in their veins, and transport in their face;
Of spirit meek, the fascinated State
With smiles our scorn shall feed, with love our hate.

Her Sons expell'd from ev'ry dear delight,
From days of pleasure, and contentment's night,
Shall toil for ever o'er the Scotish plains,
Where gloom eternal frowns, and horror reigns;
Where not a flow'r exhales its rich perfume,
And nature's blessings but in fancy bloom.
No softer springs the wand'rer's thirst supply,
Quench'd by the drops alone, which fall from high;
No simplest garden to engage their toil,
Where scarce a corner boasts the name of soil;

D   Which

Which the thin oats' thin crop can hardly rear
To feed the race of Scotfmen for the year :
In the poor limits of this wretched fpot
Themfelves, and meagre Sheep, in peace may rot.

While we each day, with lux'ry's treafures ftor'd,
Reel cloy'd and pamper'd from debauch'ry's board :
No more with craving ftomachs doom'd to feel
Th' unfinifh'd portion of a fcanty meal;
In ev'ry fleep the heaps of gold fhall glow,
Whofe ftreams, when waken'd, to our arms fhall flow,
Our cars their noify triumphs fhall difplay,
And proudly turn the Englifh from their way ;
Their midnight hours with founds of horror fhake,
And keep their very CITIZENS awake.

When call'd in crowds to bus'nefs of the ftate,
OUR facred prefence Nobles felves fhall wait ;
No more difguifing fhall the hireling chair
By liv'ry'd Bablers unattended bear ;
No grumbling mob againft our Lairdfhips fin,
Tho' plotting mifchief 'gainft themfelves within.
Yet—let the mifcreants, ever foes to right,
Survey their country's pangs with aching fight ;
On the fell authors rufh, enflam'd to ftrife,
And point their SAVAGE malice at our life;
In vain their frenzy feeks the Scotfman's fall,
OUR Soldiers, at a nod, fhall crufh them all.

3

Spite

Spite of their frown our hydra-heads afpire,
And oppofition's felf fhall mount them higher;
Holles' diminifh'd board fhall fcarce content
Thofe from c—rt kitchens by our prudence fent;
England no more luxurious treats fhall fee,
Our taftes fhall teach them Scots Simplicity;
Her lords turn'd Bankrupts fhall unpity'd fret,
Their goods, plate, chariots, glare in the Gazette;
All fix'd by purchafe in the northern god
Shall fwell the pride of his deftructive nod.

Hark how the ftorm's impetuous horror fpreads
O'er our poor kinfmens', friends', and patriots' heads;
Heap'd refignations glare adown the news,
Which difcontented hatred ftill purfues:
So rolls the torrent at N—c—le's race,
That facred p—t—ts fcarce infure a Place.
Yet full within domeftic prudence ftands,
Each faucepan guarded by her loyal hands;
Her flaves diminifh'd mourn diminifh'd fees,
And competence can fcarce the chaplains pleafe.
THESE, fighing, mourn the Novelty of tafte,
Which clips the pinions of ufurping Wafte:
With fneers prefaging that their k— muft beg,
With fruitlefs pray'r, the blefling—of an egg.

Nor here thofe dangers can the Scotfman fcore,
Which fwell the horrors of his native fhore.

Mark

Mark but at Edinburgh the manfions' fize,
Where Huts on Huts to the TENTH ftory rife ;
(Tho' now THEIR emulative ftruftures here
Bid the poor paffenger for head-piece fear)
Where tiles defcending own the ftormy wind,
(Whofe fharpeft malice Scotfmen ever find)
Which might a Valley make of Cities, fraught
With the ftarv'd Pavement they've to London brought.

'Twere well before your walks your Will to make,
(But Wills are needlefs where there's nought to take)
So frown the terrors of the bluft'ring night,
So many rattling windows to affright ;
Whofe wide-extended Jaws ne'er fail to pour
Filth's various mixtures in a copious fhower.

But, worfe than all, the Brawlers fcour the ftreet,
For Humor's fake infulting whom they meet ;
Brawlers by nature (Drunkards, I divine,
Ne'er MUCH abound without the ufe of wine)
Some mifchief ftill deep brooding in their breaft,
Who make their own by breaking others' reft:
Galba to grandeur fuch Supporters draws,
And his prime bully Verres wrefts the laws.

Yet fix'd on vengeance, tho' their rage provoke
Falfe honor's challenge for an harmlefs joke ;

The

The noble's fplendid train they wifely 'ware,
Nor prefs, like England, round a Galba's Chair.
While I, in fhades of night who rarely roam,
Who (Heav'n be thank'd) can HUG myfelf at home;
Or, if I wander, lanthorn-arm'd advance,
Like the fair partners of an Hampftead dance,
I feel his vengeance (Scotfmen all alike
At Englifhmen mechanically ftrike) .
Yet ftrike he may; I'M arm'd at heart and hand,
'Gainft ev'ry Locuft of my native land;
Avenging vigils on the Foes I keep,
Whofe tumults dare to—murder England's fleep.

Still may thefe Gods exhale with upftart pride
The ribbald ftream to NATIVE earth ally'd;
Curfe the fond nation by their Art betray'd,
" The tool of induftry, the flave of trade;
" Whofe BRUTAL courage, in the field unaw'd,
" Drops to each kingdom exercis'd in fraud;
" Then, fneering, tell me, in a wanton fport,
" Seek you my name, you'll find it at the court.
" But hence, begone, with wretches OUT OF place
" For Scotfmen thus to parly, is difgrace:
" While our own laird the full-blown rev'rence draws,
" And WISE as VIRTUOUS confecrates our caufe.
" Yet, England, with thy doom contented fit,
" Thofe ONCE who quit us muft for EVER quit:

" OUR

" Our loyal zéal the fcripture-doctrine proves,

" Who moves NOT FOR US, HE AGAINST US moves."

   Ill-fated kingdom, where corruption's note
Plants her relentlefs dagger at thy throat ;
Or, when each fav'ring avenue is barr'd,
Can fteal her poifon thro' a flumb'ring guard ;
Oft her delufive inftruments advance,
Fann'd to deftruction by the breath of France ;
Bid the full glories of our conquefts ceafe,
Ufurp our dear-bought rights, and mock with peace ;
Thus ev'ry nation wooes us but to cheat,
And vanquifh'd foes ftill triumph when they treat.

   And yet experience boafts our fpotlefs times,
Which curfe the mighty heap of former crimes ;
While fewer dungeons NOW fuffice the town,
Improv'd in tafte by Ludgates taken down.
Thus flufh'd with virtues, my prophetic mufe
(Nor long fhall fancy only feaft her views)
My mufe proclaims a happier fall by far,
The fall, ye Scotifh fwains, of Temple-Bar.

   More folid caufes might my courfe delay,
But facred judgment beckons me away ;
Judgment, whofe fober mandate checks my fire,
And fmiles no more my Satire to infpire.

                                       But

But thou, oh ! ———, on whofe fteady foul
The beams of friendfhip blaze with full control,
From learning's feat, indulgent genius, deign
To point my venom, and enlarge my ftrain;
To roll with animated force the ftream,
O'erflow'd with gall, when Scotland is my theme.

THE

THE

FOURTH SATIRE

IMITATED*.

HENCE, Vice, begone; 'gainſt thee enrag'd I
   wing
 My daring flight, and point the ſatire's ſting:
Thou fiend, ſtill carelefs of the voice of fame,
Still unreclaim'd by virtue's heav'nly flame;
Alike my foe, whatever paſſion guide
Thy tainted ſoul, ambition, luſt, or pride.
Ah! what avail the ſplendors of the ſtar,
The bounding courfers, or the rattling car?

---

* The ſubjeƈt of this imitation is an anecdote in our Englifh hiſtories,
of the moſt ridiculous nature; which is here the more amply enlarged on,
as it ſerves to prove (in a prepoſterous farce, unneceſſarily carry'd on by a
Tyrant) the very near affinity betwixt folly and oppreſſion.

             Ah!

Ah ! what avails the manfion high difplay'd,
Like Lux'ry's temple 'mid th' incumbent fhade ?
Their awful lord fhould plenteous acres own,
He builds on fordid dirt a weak renown :
The frown of Satire checks his wanton boaft,
Tho' thoufand virgins mourn their virtue loft.

But now, defcending from the height of crimes,
Survey the vicious follies of the times ;
Which fpread from MODEST priefthood o'er the land,
Well need the cenfure of correction's hand.

Hear ruthlefs Mauro, with faftidious plan
(Nor deem profeffion confecrates the man)
On fpotlefs virtue fell detraction roll,
For errors rankling in his coarfer foul ;
Whofe horrid bronze as horrid features GRACE,
His bofom's blacknefs frowning in his face :
Hear him with wat'ring mouth, and panting heart,
Great mafter of the culinary art,
Bawl the rich lecture to the prieftly train,
And deathlefs triumphs from his nonfenfe gain.
Whofe prudence pure, untinctur'd with deceit,
Not, Lowther-like, in waggons heaps the treat,
But STEALS his ribbald fcrawls to grandeur's arms,
When high ambition wooes the Mitre's charms.

Ev'n now he grafps the vifionary prize,
And, flufh'd with fecond fpring, to * beauty flies:
A ftern bafhaw in love, whofe law's his will,
While felf, felf only is the miftrefs ftill.
And is it thus that pride's affected tool,
Who forms from venal eftimates his rule,
Who ftruts in trappings from his country torn,
And eyes each fcrible, but his own, with fcorn;
To mufic low'rs the felf-fufficient grin,
Without one fpark of harmony within,
Is't thus that Mauro, lur'd by plenty's bowl,
Loaths the dull tafk, the bufinefs of the foul;
His feft'ring paffion truth nor manners tie,
He talks, writes, preaches, ev'n from vanity.;
To rude buffoon'ry facrifices fenfe;
At feafts alone his happy Refidence;
While to his boaft tafte, learning, genius fall,
In thought the true coloffus o'er us all.

* The genuine difpofition of the character here defcribed may be con-
jectured from the following epigram:

    By Shaft'fbury's fancy 'twas of late exprefs'd,
    That only ridicule's of truth the teft:
    This rev'rend cenfure views, and fcorns to own
    The fhallow tyrant lifted to the throne;
    Such zeal for truth from books to life extends,
    And fondly fooths his difappointed ends;
    While fcandal's manlier ftrains his rancor move
    To blaft the fair he cannot win to love.

Away,

Away, ye facred nine! celeftial maids!
Still roam embofom'd in your fecret fhades;
I call no virgins to Britannia's plain,
To point my fatire, and infpire my ftrain.

When brutal Mary fway'd the Englifh helm,
And bloody popery ravag'd all the realm,
The mother's fancy'd load opprefs'd the queen;
——Fair virtue with a figh furveys the fcene:
Still lies fhe penfive in the arms of pain,
As real labor from th' embrace of Spain.

Falfe zeal in rapture views the ling'ring hope,
Whofe birth infures a vaffal to the Pope;
If others' pray'rs a diff'rent prince require,
The Papift rages with indignant fire,
And hurries, frantic for religion's fake,
Th' unhappy victims martyrs to the ftake.
Should' others' voice the fond affent deny,
As Mary's ficknefs were a ftatefman's lie,
Forth rufh th' informing tribe, with rigid flame,
Fir'd at this infult on their monarch's name.
" Say whence the jeft," they cry, " the fcoffing mirth,
" On all that's beauty, and on all that's worth?
" Beware the founds, which princely anger draw,
" Nor ftain the bulwark of the church and law;
" Left vengeance rifing check the thoughtlefs breath,
" Nor leave to ficknefs' pains the work of death.

" And

" And know, opprobrious, from the hand of pow'r
" The wing'd revenge will haften to devour;
" Then, vainly then, in life's laft tortures mourn,
" That e'er your madnefs dar'd a queen to fcorn."

Now to the palace with devouring fight,
Where all are welcome, who are foes to right,
Prefs the full crowd;—firft eager Gardiner flies,
As the lov'd mitre's charms allur'd his eyes;
" Hail, happy morn, thrice-hail, diftinguifh'd day,
" Shine forth, bright Phœbus, with redoubled ray;
" Ye fons of popery, bid adieu to care;
" Now pious * Princefs, and your train defpair;
" Spring, fpring to life, and guide, celeftial youth,
" Each wand'ring foul to pop'ry, and to truth."

Frail grandeur fwell'd with flatt'ry's giddy line
Quits the low earth, and foars to the divine;
A chofen band fhe fummons to debate,
Some from her love, and others from her hate;
Such diff'rent natures form the motley fhew,
As various colors fpread the heav'nly bow.

Wrap'd in the facred prelate's foberer veft,
Ill-fuited to his favage brutal breaft,
Firft rufhes Bonner with impatient breath,
" Now, now, my brethren, to the work of death;"

* Q. Elizabeth.

The

The chief of flaughter's fiends he glows to fill
Each hour with terror, and inhuman ill:
At Mary's nod, in Popery's hellifh caufe,
He ftamps on right, and tramples o'er the laws.

Mildnefs in heart, in form a papift, *Pole*
I view with pitying, yet revering foul;
Lov'd of the tyrant queen to him belong
Sweetnefs of mind, and elegance of tongue:
When the fell favage's inhuman breaft
Prepar'd each fharpeft pang to Virtue's reft,
How oft THY milder notes the ftream withftood,
Nor wifh'd Religion's footfteps mark'd with blood!
The wretch obeys, fufpends th' ungen'rous toil,
And Mary's felf compaffion learns a-while.
Oh! hadft thou bid the ftorm for ever ceafe,
And lull'd her bofom to RELIGIOUS peace;
The mufe had dar'd the heav'nly deed commend,
And thou, where Cranmer fail'd, hadft prov'd a friend.

In profp'ring ftate with richeft bleffings fpread,
Thus Pole the council's chief, the church's head,
At length in hoary grace, with peaceful doom,
Sunk, like the patriarch, to the welcome tomb.

Not fo great Cranmer, who with virtuous zeal
Breath'd, acted, dy'd for his religion's weal;
With good old Latimer's foft-fmiling age,
And dauntlefs Ridley, venerable fage,

He

He fcorns the tyrant's frown, the tort'ring ftake,
And falls juft falt'ring for religion's fake.
What now avails, that with unfhaken hand
He fcatter'd truth, and virtue o'er the land?
What now avails, that with fuccefsful fway
He form'd young Edward to the golden way?
Vain is the preacher's glow, th'inftructor's pride,
Cranmer, and virtue funk, when Edward dy'd.

To thefe a meagre pallid number came,
The flaves of vices, and unknown to fhame;
Worn out in crimes, yet reeking with perfume,
To give fome graces to a fhatter'd bloom;
Scarce animated ghofts, whofe bodies find
A proper femblance in an ill-form'd mind;
Spaniels of court, who with a fupple grace
Smile at their foes, and whifper friends from place.

Now flowly ftalks in furly grandeur great
The would-be tyrant of each church and ftate;
Tyrant of England then, but foon to moan
His ravifh'd pow'r from great Eliza's throne.
Oh! how the monfter fucks with greedy eyes
For future years the tributary prize!
Poor blinded wretch, who views the time no more,
When Henry drove him from the Englifh fhore.
The future flave he fees with mad delight;
The flave, in what his frenzy terms the right;

Tranf-

Tranſported, as when princes leave their home,
To pay due homage at HIS feet in Rome.

Th' ungovern'd legate fan'd with fiercer fires
A ſtream of wild enthuſiaſt zeal inſpires;
The deſp'rate Minion ſtorms with brutal rage,
Nor ſtays his eager curſe from ſex, or age:
" Now, happy Rome, a waſte of joy diſplay,
" And own the bleſſings of this genial day;
" A madden'd Henry's rigid frown no more
" Shall wreſt your precepts from this ſubjeſt ſhore;
" This day for ever bends to pop'ry's reign
" At once the Britons, and the ſons of Spain,
" I ſee, I ſee, in richeſt ſplendors riſe
" Each future aſtion to my conſcious eyes;
" His gen'rous ſoul a full-blown greatneſs bears,
" To deck the monarch for a length of years;
" Burſt from the narrow limits of the womb,
" Ariſe, my Prince, and for a nation bloom."

Now, friends, cries Bonner with fanatic zeal,
Fix the dread ſtake, prepare the tort'ring wheel;
From hence, where'er the regal footſteps tread,
Be ev'ry place with bleeding ſubjeſts ſpread.

Thus ſpoke the fiend; the threats of brutal ire
The good deteſt, and papiſts ſcarce admire:

But

But he ftill thirfts to try the murd'rous art,
And fhow'r fell torments on the human heart;
" In Edward's days ye trod fecure of harm,
" For vig'rous counfels ftop'd my daring arm;
" No Pope in fetters bound the vaffal-realm,
" No carelefs Spaniard flumber'd at the helm:
" But now 'tis pafs'd, I tread deftruction's way,
" And the heart loves, when once it taftes the prey."

Thus, after nothing done, the council rife,
Victims alike of terror and furprize;
The papift train with daring taunts purfue,
And low'r defiance to the virtuous few;
With confcious joy, as Mary's gracelefs reign
Had bent ftol'n Calais to her yoke again.

Thus had fhe pafs'd the moments of her life
In giddy trifles, and fantaftic ftrife,
What facred prelates had furviv'd to grace,
And fpread rich glories on a future race!
Unknown to harm the guiltlefs reign had ftood,
Not ftamp'd with carnage, and embru'd in blood:—
Yet heav'n beheld—the fcepter'd mifcreant lyes,—
Detefted victim to religion's cries.

E   THE

THE

FIFTH SATIRE

IMITATED.

WHAT! ftill dependent on the flaves of ftate,
Still doft thou haunt the tables of the great?
Tho' ceafelefs infults fmite thee to the face,
Which had incens'd ev'n Wolfey in difgrace.
Away; no more thefe giddy joys purfue;
All nature's wants, believe me, are but few;
And richer blifs contentment's fmiles afford,
Than crowns the plenty of a noble's board.

Ah! rather fhudd'ring in the face of day,
Go, at fome road thy menial wants difplay;
Go, rummage all the magazine of woes,
The broken leg, the fhiver'd arm difclofe;

On

On fome dry'd bone, the dog's detefted treat,
Let thy teeth labor for the fcrap of meat;
Groan the long night, earth only for thy bed,
While low'ring tempefts break above thy head;
This rather be thy lot, than flave of pelf
Sell for a bribe thy virtue, and thy felf;
Or live the Mercury of an upftart's breaft,
By fmiles elated, and by frowns deprefs'd.

But lo! the blifsful hour arrives at laft,
A full reward for all thy labors paft;
My lord fteps forth,—" To-morrow I wou'd fee
" Florio at dinner;—know, I dine at three."
Hence, care (thou cry'ft) hence, forrow, to the wind,
I will be happy, for my lord is kind.—
Alas! no kindnefs rules the noble's will,—
He knows not elfe an empty chair to fill;—
Perhaps by Florio's prefence he intends
T'improve the laughter of his neighb'ring friends.

But thou elate with madnefs of delight
Know'ft not to fleep a fingle wink at night;
Such fond expectance flutters in thy head,
Thou fly'ft in confcious tranfport from thy bed;
Thro' the deep midnight poring to furvey,
If yet the fun-beams ufher in the day;—
At length, exulting at the rifing dawn,
Thy toiling eyes falute the happy morn.

( )   Lo!

Lo! Florio now, array'd in all his beſt,
(Leſt my good lord ſhould think him meanly dreſs'd)
Impatient ruſhing Becket's ſhrine to greet,
Thanks his kind ſtars, if foremoſt of the treat.

But hark! what fury! what envenom'd ſtrains!
As ſome dire frenzy had inflam'd your brains:
Whence fly with giddy rage the maſſy bowls,
As more than carnivals infpir'd your ſouls!
Whence does this blood diſtain thy mangled face!
And the ſpilt cups thy reeking breaſt diſgrace!
Whence, but ſubſervient to thy patron's will,
Enflaming wines thy madden'd boſom fill!
And now thou roar'ſt inebriate with thy joys,
Till Becket's frown ſpeaks ſilence to the noiſe:
Yet know, 'tis well, ſupremely bleſs'd thy doom,
If the ſlave thruſts not Florio from the room.

Add that the noble feaſts his mirthful vein
With the rich-ſparkling treaſures of Champagne:
For him Burgundia's fertil region pours
With laviſh finger all her choiceſt ſtores:
For him Italia's luxury rears the vine;
His the rich tribute of Oporto's wine,
Which flow'd unrival'd, fanctify'd by age,
Ere France enervated the nation's rage.
Far different draughts thy meaner lot await—
Think not to ſip preſumptuous with the great;

Contented

Contented to thy lot if wines fhould fall
Adult'rate, four, or ANY wine at all.

Lo! fmiling Becket with luxurious foul
Triumphant grafps the gold-encircled bowl;
Or the rich diamond's pride in coftly rows
Around the ftudded cup refplendent glows;
This may thine eyes at awful diftance fee,
More were prophane, the fight's enough for thee.
But fhou'd thy patron with indulgent mind
Grant thee a touch (ah! that indeed were kind!)
The flaves with watchful eye the cup behold,
The diamonds count, and pore upon the gold.
For thee (enough thy menial hands to deck)
The narrow HORN extends its crany neck;
Thro' this to fuck the vine's poor fparing juice,
And know, 'tis well if cleans'd for Florio's ufe.
Should the gout's flighteft torment pain my lord
(The well-known vifitant of grandeur's board)
His circling minions richeft cordials feize
To footh the wretch to temporary eafe.
Faft by thy fide the negro takes his ftand,
And fills thy aukward cup with brawny hand;
A wretch, who met amid the gloom of night
Would fill thy foul with horror and affright;
Left while thou trod'ft the folitary way,
Like the Venetian, he might ftab for pay.

For him the youths in liv'ry'd pride array'd,
Expert and ſkilful in the HANDY trade,
Shine round the board, and wait his lordly call,—
The flow'r, the glory of the ſlaves of Gaul;
Slaves the thin joys of native air who leave,
Thy laviſh plenty, England, to receive,]
Dare not on theſe a lordly eye to turn;
They curſe thy mandate, and thy cries they ſpurn:
Not ſuch to thee the laughing bowl impart,
Too well, alas! they know thee, who thou art.
Not ſuch, neglectful of their titled lord,
Skip to THY voice, and dance around thy board;—
Thee, menial gueſt, with grudging eye they view,
A gueſt the meaner vaſſal of the two.

With equal ſway among the lordly great
Pride rules the kitchen, and the rooms of ſtate:
While ſparing ſcraps thy tortur'd tooth engage,
Stiffen'd and moulder'd with a length of age,
White as the ſnow before my lord is ſpread
(Who nips with tender tooth) the ſofteſt bread;
Away; nor dare extend thy longing hand;
In vain (as ignorant of the dread command)
In vain thou plead'ſt the wiſhes of thine eyes,
A ſlave ſtands o'er, and wreſts the ſmiling prize.
" Perverſe, preſumptuous, wilt thou never find
" What's for my lord, and what's for thee deſign'd?

" T

" This for thy touch 'twere madnefs to intend—
" Such treafures only blefs a TITLED friend."

Was it for this (thy murmuring voice may cry)
I dar'd the rigors of th'inclement fky?
For this deferted all the fweets of life,
My happier cottage, and my fonder wife?
For this, while ev'ry eye was clos'd in fleep,
Toil'd o'er the midnight hill's afpiring fteep?
For this?—and ftill frail fortune's fordid tool,
Thou liv'ft the vaffal of an upftart fool.

See, for proud Becket fhow'rs the willing main
The richeft glories of her finny train;
For him the pike extends, aufpicious lord,
Its monarch bulk upon the fplendid board;
High rear'd above, the joys luxurious fee,
It tow'rs in grandeur, and looks down on THEE;
Not this thy treat, not thine the royal fifh,
Blefs'd if the FARMER'S FARE adorn thy difh:
His tafte the richeft fauce exuberant greets,
And fheds in laughing ftreams its fragrant fweets:
For thee the bafelefs oil, whofe fteamy light
Spreads its dim influence on the face of night.

For Becket's lips the turtle's fweets attend,
Which to his board the rifled Indies fend;
For him the huntfman's care, the fifher's toil,
'The plains they ravage, and the feas they fpoil;

For

For him with gaping fearch th' expectant heir
Ranfacks the wing'd inhabitants of air;
Difdainful of the Law, whofe milder pow'r
Protracts from fons of fport their little hour.
Whilft thou, the flave, the victim of difgrace,
Pin'ft 'mid th' encircling joys of plenty's face;
And ftill, clofe-fetter'd, hug'ft thy menial ftate,
Thefe fmiles of woe, this ftarving with the great.

   Yet hear, ye nobles, and attend the ftrain
Of independent virtue's dauntlefs train:
" What mean th' infulting frowns, the fcornful eyes,
" UNTITLED goodnefs daring to defpife?
" Think'ft thou, we deign to afk, prefumptuous lord,
" The various largefs, or perpetual board?
" Think'ft thou with flatt'ry's cringing ftep we roam
" To thee, UNABLE of the feaft at home?
" Know, that thou feeft the man, whofe gen'rous foul
" No grandeur frights, no menaces control;
" Know, that thou hear'ft the voice, whofe daring ftrain
" Will anfwer threat for threat, for fcorn difdain:
" Nor think, fubfervient to thy lordly call,
" As flaves to fcourge us, or as vaffals gall;
" The manly bofom is, and will be free;
" Or treat with kindnefs, or invite not me.
" Still let the Parafite thy treat commend,
" Still praife voracious, whom he thinks his friend;

" Still

" Still may he cry (dependent on thy fmile)
" Let peafants hunger, and let oxen toil ;
" The world around me rul'd by fortune's pow'r,
" Or feel the adverfe, or the profp'rous hour ;
" Others I heed not, if the great afford
" The lavifh plenty of his friendly board."

Meanwhile th' unllv'ry'd fop (by mode of town
Whofe ufelefs ftation claims him HALF-A-CROWN)
If once neglected, with a well-bred grace,
Affronts the guefts, and ftares them in the face :
Urg'd by his nod (how envy'd is thy doom !)
The noify flaves rufh joftling o'er the room :
Alas! what boots the head's afflictive pain ?
Be ftill, licentious, for thou mourn'ft in vain.
The tool of grandeur with a ceafelefs fmart
Muft bear each infult of the head, and heart ;
Muft fuffer (happy if no ills befide)
The jefts of folly, and the ftings of pride.

But ftill, vain Florio, ftill wilt thou defcry
The world's falfe fplendors with a jaundic'd eye ?
Did ever lordly Becket deign to fip
The cup polluted by thy meaner lip ?
Did ever Florio with a free-born foul
With Becket dare to crown the mutual bowl ?
Or from his voice the friendly accents prove,
" Here's health and tranfport to the man I love ?"

Ah !

Ah! no fuch founds thy flavifh ftation blefs;
Thine—to be filent, till he deigns addrefs.
And Becket; well thou know'ft, with diff'rent face
Eyes the plain veftment, and the dazzling lace.

But fay, fhould heav'n with arm indulgent fhow'r
The beaming charms of riches, or of pow'r,
What fmiling fcenes thy vary'd ftate would crown!
No more the menial flave of Becket's frown;
No more devoted to this earthly god
Would Florio ftoop, and tremble at a nod;
Each milder found wou'd ftream from Becket's breaft,
" Thou deareft brother, and moft welcome gueft;"
Now fhining high in grandeur, fame, and birth,
Tho' late the refufe, and the dregs of earth.
" Come then, my friend, unknowing of control,
" With all my plenty feaft thy lib'ral foul;
" Come, 'tis for thee the lavifh banquet's fpread,
" Slave, to my friend the full-brim'd goblet fhed."

Accurfed gold! array'd in friendfhip's veft,
Deluding flatt'ry feeds thy votary's breaft;
Know then, exalted, 'tis thy fordid pelf,
That gains the fmile of grandeur, not thy felf.

'Tis not enough that wealth thy bofom grace,
If thine the bleffings of the lifping race;

Not round thy board with prattling voice muſt run
The beauteous daughter, or the dearer ſon.
If fortune frown, thy teeming wife may bear
The welcome burden each revolving year;
Then Becket's ſelf with tender voice may deign
With little gifts to ſooth the wanton train;
Himſelf admiring of the harmleſs joys,
Pour from his hand the rattles, and the toys:
The infant there the fondeſt friend will find,
Where no expeſtant hopes o'er-rul'd the mind.

The KINDRED muſhroom on his nod attends,
While frowns the TOAD-STOOL on inferior friends:
He feaſts indiff'rent, ſhould they eat or faſt,
Indiff'rent, tho' this morſel were their laſt.

See now, reclining on the chair of ſtate,
He ſmiles indulgent o'er the neighb'ring great;
For them the laviſh pine does luxury bring
From manſions cheriſh'd with eternal ſpring;
And richeſt fruits (for ſuch alone ſuffice)
Bid the taſte revel in the ſweets of ice.
Thus grandeur tow'rs with whims fantaſtic grac'd,
'Tis thine to feed thy noſtrils, not thy taſte;
At beſt but doom'd with thankful ſmile to eat
Some deaden'd WIND-FALL for thy ſordid treat;
Such on parades the rude recruits devour,
Who play with muſquets at a ſerjeant's pow'r.

The

The great he welcomes; but with ceaseless smart
He toils to fill thy agonizing heart;
Studious the scene of laughter to display,
And send thee famish'd from the long-wish'd day:
This Becket's will; and just thy slavish doom,
Thou laughter, scorn, and OUTLAW of the room.

Go, shameless votary to inglorious pelf,
Florio, away, and learn to know thy self:
Tho' " mine (thou cry'st) the bold undaunted breast,
" With all my country's honest freedom bless'd;
" Mine the firm heart, ne'er hush'd to mean control;"—
Yet Becket spies the liar in thy soul;
Yes, all thy fears he views, and knows thee well,
Lull'd by the fragrance of the kitchen's smell.

Who else regardless of th' insulting strain
Would hug the charms of slav'ry's menial chain;
Nor dare to pour resentment's headlong tide,
And quash the frown of grandeur and of pride?
Heav'ns! should my bosom haunt the noble's treat,
If fed with moulder'd scraps of sordid meat,
While at the board a neighb'ring guest employs
His feasting palate with luxurious joys?
Would I, vain flatt'rer! bear with patient breast
(Spurn'd like the brute) the slave's inhuman jest?
No; my soul, fearless of the titled lord,
Would spurn his favors, and detest his board.

Away

Away then; grandeur's tyrant-heart defpife,
Enflam'd by virtue's call to vengeance rife :
Go, when he frowns, thy injur'd bofom free,
And point the diff'rence 'twixt a flave and thee.
But if, allur'd by bafe corruption's charms,
Thou hug'ft difhonor with a lover's arms,
Still may'ft thou bear contempt's eternal fong,
And all the venom of a noble's tongue !
Still live they victims of opprobrious fhame,
Whofe bofoms triumph in the lofs of fame !
Ne'er, ne'er to THESE th' injurious infult end,
When SUCH the banquet, and when SUCH the friend.

THE

THE

SIXTH SATIRE

IMITATED.

YE S—o'er the world in Adam's earlier days
Thou pour'd'ft, fair Chaftity, thy lenient rays:
Yes—ftill they fhone refplendent o'er the mind,
When fimpler mortals, to the hut confin'd,
Smil'd in their houfhold's comfortable fhade,
Alike to fhepherds, and to flocks difplay'd.
Th' unpolifh'd confort then fecurely prefs'd
Her verdant pillow wrap'd in balmy reft;
While hides and leaves their canopy difpenfe,
To fhield the lids of flumb'ring innocence:
No lap-dog's pains her eye with tears defile,
No hufband's death extracts the willing fmile.

Then

Then ſtrod the ſturdy ſwain in honeſt pride,
His healthy infants prattling by his ſide;
And the fond partner, with unborrow'd grace,
Shews happy union beaming in her face:
Forms truly great, of nature's genuine clay,
Not ſprung like muſhrooms of a modern day.

Then ſhone, O Modeſty! thy bleſs'd domain;
Few traces left in ancient David's reign,
When the meek lambkin's too-alluring charm
Fell to the rapine of the monarch's arm;
No need of juſtice the foul crime to ſcan,
A Nathan's voice to conſcience points—the man:
Now juſtice has to law the throne reſign'd,
And ſhame takes ſhelter but in folly's mind.

Old Time a ſanction on the mode has ſhed,
Which blaſts the tranſports of the nuptial bed;
In other deeds we brazen years behold;
In this—the age of luxury and gold.

But lo! the parchment-chain, the lawyer's zeal,
The treach'rous friend, the witneſs, and the ſeal,
Stamp the fair ſcene of bliſs; gay Strephon ſtands
Juſt ſpruc'd, and monkey'd from the barber's hands;
Long has the preſent ſmil'd with winning art,
Till the laſt ling'ring gift inſures the heart.

Say,

Say, giddy ftripling, what o'er-ruling fire
Enflames thy bofom to the wild defire?
Can no amufement lend its friendly aid?
See Arthur's ever-open doors difplay'd;
Matrons and Methodifts with routs engage,
A Bridge with Latin, and with farce the ftage.
Go then, unfetter'd with a hufband's care,
Nor wifh the earlier profpect of an heir;
Still let expectant kinfmen fhed their ftores,
Or the more fawning friend befiege thy doors;
Some clouded Jefuit, who with crafty rule
Commands your pockets, and proclaims you fool.
Hence, fon of pleafure, whofe ungovern'd life
Muft feel the rein to fit thee for a wife;
For fmiles from virtue's charms you vainly ftrive,
Who ftoop with threefcore years at twenty-five.

Are virtue's charms for libertines defign'd?
For thee the faultlefs frame, the fpotlefs mind?—
'Tis wifdom's tafk to bend before the fhrine,
That tafk, which folly makes thee wifh for thine.
Thro' private life who moves with fteady grace;
Who dares the fcandal of a public place;
On whom no cenfures rev'rend dotards fhed;
But dwell delighted on the NAT'RAL RED;
Such calls for blifs, for bleffings on the fair
Pour forth, ye friends, the tributary pray'r,

F   That

That nuptial vows increafing pledges bring,
To fhare the tranfports which from goodnefs fpring.

Enflam'd by love, from England's hated air,
Flies with the flutt'ring lord the courtly fair;
From fcene to fcene fhe roams with fond delight,
Till Bremen's friendly feat retards her flight.
Thus, while the matron with a fneering fmile
Weeps o'er her tea th' intemp'rance of the ifle,
SHE, with her reftlefs partner, leaves behind
Houfe, parents, kindred, with contented mind;
In vain the kind defpondents wifh her ftay,
In vain the dearer op'ra, ball, or play.
Ah! what avails, from plenty's foft'ring hand
She taftes indulgence at a fire's command:
She fpurns the low'ring ftorm, the ftings of fhame,
Nor heeds, when love forbids, the call of fame.
Survey her fmiling with undaunted foul,
While the rough ocean's angry billows roll;
Ah! little thinking fhe may fhortly prove
Far greater tempefts on the SEA of love.

Say, marry'd dames, would no evafions fire
Refiftance to a hufband's fond defire?
No fhifts of cunning to divert his fight;
No mimic'd ftumble, or no cold to fright?
Magicians fly, whofe fertil fancies form
At will a fky ferene, or threat'ning ftorm.

Bold

Bold as the maiden, mount the giddy ſhip,
Go, brave the dangers of the roaring deep:
Nor ſickneſs' qualms, nor nauſeous ſmells offend
The heart thus center'd in a faithful friend.
Go, chat familiar by the ſailor's ſide,
With all the ſtripling's condeſcending pride.

See the bold knight with captivating ſmiles
In comely youth the yielding fair beguiles;
His the clear luſtre of a blooming face,
Where ev'ry feature ſtrikes with ſofteſt grace:
Mark the quick ear, the piercing eye, with awe,
And keep ſuch treaſures from a foreign Spaw.
How ſure of tranſport is the nuptial plan,
When kindred title ſanctifies the man;
Title, whoſe radiance ſpeaks with dazzling glare,
" Go, riſe ſuperior to the ſiſter-fair:"
Seek ye the reſt?—His virtues and his fame
Let the poor relics of a club proclaim.

What nuptial joys diſcordant boſoms cheer,
Learn from th' example of a fondling peer:
Repeated rivals form his day's delight,
And ſolitary ſlumbers crown the night:
SHE, won by faſhion's more prevailing charms,
For ev'ry upſtart leaves his drowſy arms;
With one congenial nymph inur'd to roam,
Nor, till her gold's exhauſted, thinks of HOME.

F 2   Enflam'd

Enflam'd the widow's faded joys to prove,
Pam gaily flutters with th' alarms of love;
No need of charms to fafcinate the heart,
When wealth's fuperior luftre points the dart.
Let vacant coxcombs to the fair indite
Their am'rous nonfenfe, tho' they fcarce can write;
Yet happier fhe by far whofe fate has try'd
The widow's freedom in the fondled bride.

How funk Florello's foul, to love betray'd!
Sunk to thofe beauties which fo quickly fade!
When from confumption's undermining pow'r,
A meagre ghoft fhe lies in ficknefs' hour,
Then vary'd low'rs the note: " Thou flave of art,
" Thy form departed ftings me to the heart;
" That fhrivell'd corfe befits the mould'ring tomb,—
" Hence—others wait my fmile in beauty's bloom."
Yet fhe at pleafure's call could wafte away
Her gold at Deard's, her fpirits at a play;
Whate'er o'er London's fpace attracts her eyes,
Plate, jewels, laces, ev'ry thing fhe buys:
This the fole value of her fleeting pelf,
To leave no neighbor to outvie herfelf.

In thefe fad times, when low'ring to the eyes
The faithful Gazette teems with bankruptcies,
Each pageant lux'ry decks the trader's wife,
How elfe fupported were a city-life?

The

The diamond's heap pil'd o'er an aukward mien
To make her worthy to falute a queen ;
Jewels, which handed down by antient rule,
New fet for fafhion, fhine from fool to fool ;
Doom'd to fome duchefs' pride their borrow'd ray,
When fmiles a gaping coronation-day ;
Unlefs at pawn their melancholy place,
Lodg'd with the fneaking fwine-detefting race.

If thine the wifhes of CONNUBIAL chains,
Where birth fuperior dignifies the veins ;
Where virtue prompts each action of the mind,
Like gentle England much to peace inclin'd ;
There bind the knot ; the phœnix checks my rage,
When thus our boarding-fchools adorn the age.

Sure the worft torment of the marry'd life
Is confcious merit in a titled wife :
Be mine a ftranger to the modes of town—
Thefe faultlefs wives the name of hufband drown,
What is to me the brother's martial fire ?
Let him and all his tricks to camp retire :
If kindred ties the minifterial great,
I wifh him happy with his load of ftate.

Hence, fcandal, hence divert thy poifon'd darts,
Nor fpend their guilty rage on harmlefs hearts.

Thus

Thus Juftice cries : One female errs alone ;
Why blaft 'the reft for errors not their own ?
In vain ; like quickfilver the demon runs,
Piercing the fame of parents, daughters, fons ;
Each friend an upftart, that at wealth's command
Looks big as fhe who lords it o'er the Strand.

Thus heav'nly virtues languifh in the fair,
Dazzled by vanity's fantaftic glare,
Whofe baneful flames each focial tranfport pall,
And turn the fweetnefs of the foul to gall.

Should fuch a confort blefs man's happier choice,
Tho' fome faint praifes flutter on his voice,
Her folid worth how trivial muft he deem !
For where's the force of love without efteem ?

One leffer fault the cens'ring ftrains impart,
Small, tho' a torment to the hufband's heart :
Whence fprings, ye fair, the paffion of the mind,
Which good, nor beauty, but from France can find ?
In foreign founds how ill is knowledge fhewn,
While, very Englifh, ignorant of your own !
Why to exprefs refentment, fear, or joy,.
Muft the full bofom ftranger-words employ ?
Why too in French muft ev'ry SECRET roll ?
(Go next and truft them to a Frenchman's foul)

Such

Such, man, avoid !—oh ! fave the parfon's fee;
The hand unite not, where the heart is free.

When fuch the wife, fhe fways with boundlefs pow'r ;
A flave I hail you from the nuptial hour.
Ope wide the purfe-ftrings, let the treafures fly,
Some trinket, or fome monkey ftrikes her eye :
If jealous, fhe will vex you all fhe can ;
They've num'rous arts to plague a loving man.
A very cypher the fond hufband ftands ;
To buy, or fell, all paffes thro' her hands.
New friendfhips fhe will form, while thofe before,
Whom moft you lov'd, are driven from the door.
Mean while infipid aunts, and Yorkfhire coufins,
With UPSTART uncles, fhe admits by dozens;
And if the world approv'd, her fondling care
Would fix fome former fuitor for thy heir.

Now to the kitchen : There fupreme her rule ;
My lady's maid chief ufher of the fchool.
Your older fervants firft fhe turns away,
For thofe a miftrefs care not to obey :
Afk you their faults ? I will (fhe cries) prevail!
And pins a faucy difh-clout to your tail.
Thee and thy fervants too fhe views with fcorn,
Nor thinks fuch wretches like herfelf were born.

Tir'd

Tir'd for awhile of tyranny at home,
Now to a neighbor-friend her footſteps roam ;
A friend, when abſent, at whoſe faults ſhe ſneers,
She courts to ſet her houſhold by the ears ;
Leaving her dear expectant lord the while,
Tho' yet the HONEY-MOON around them ſmile.
Thus, ever-reſtleſs, toils ſhe till her doom,
When " hic quieſcit " greets him on her tomb.

The fierceſt ſtorms, that nuptial peace offend,
Riſe from th'intruſion of a BOSOM FRIEND.
This boſom friend, deny it if you can,
Diſplays her love by hatred to the man ;
Unleſs herſelf procureſs ; then each ſnare
Is ſpread t' entrance the virtue of the fair ;
She puffs her pretty thing with rapt'rous voice,
And damns the freedom of a better choice.
From ſuch, ye parents, guard the filial breaſt ;
They all are W—f—ds *, and with frauds poſſeſs'd :
W—f—ds, whoſe ſmile's inſinuating ray
Throws the coy maiden in the lover's way,
Directs th' unwilling hand the lines to ſuit
To dying ſtriplings, hurrying to recruit ;
Who boaſt, that lap-dogs can inſure a heart,
And break the truſt, repos'd thro' OTHERS' art.

* The name of an obſcure woman ; not a well-known enthuſiaſt among
the Methodiſts.

When

When riots in the houfe alarm the play'r,
Pity the fofter fex fhould venture there : .
Can fwords and blood the female foul delight?
Or the torn bench give tranfport to the fight?
Hail, patriot-heroines, whofe o'er-ruling call
May ftill infure a Chinefe Feftival ;
May at a frown bid Garrick's humbler tide
To deep Fitz——k's eloquence fubfide.

What calm amufements female hours beguile
Some future fale will tell us with a fmile ;
The lots difpos'd,—in parcell'd order come
The dancing-habit, race-horfe, pipe, and drum ;
Perhaps to dazzle beaux they'll lift the fhield,
When warrior-Joans head Britain to the field.

In fummer, what a load the lighteft veft !
And yet their only comfort's—to be drefs'd.
Afk to what ufe the hoop's extended pride,
When courtly thoufands prefs on ev'ry fide ;
When joftled here, and there, before, behind,
She turns to all, as vanes before the wind :
In other fcenes fhe'd faint without fupport ;—
There can be nothing, but muft pleafe at court.
Th' unfriendly weight (thank Heav'n !) falutes the day,
By mode doom'd only for the court or play.

Their

Their baneful gall when cold fufpicions fhed,
How fwell the forrows of the marriage-bed !
Yet art's kind fuccor checks the hufband's flame,
The fair with fighs deceitful clears her fhame :
She brands the children that from him were born,
Then rolls the torrent with inverted fcorn ;
Nay threatens, in her fame's defence, to prove
Where her good cenfor fought forbidden love :
Grief ftops her voice; the tears, inceffant flood,
Flow down her cheek in melancholy mood ;
Tears, faithful vaffals to the female fkill—
They boaft, that they can laugh or weep at will.
You, fondling Damon, with th' abfolving kifs
Convicted prefs the object of your blifs :
Go to her papers ; there the proofs you'll find.—
Go, blefs the banquets to an eafy mind.

Whence fpring thefe evils, dreadful to behold ?
Serener quiet chear'd our fons of old :
Then fmil'd each partner with his faithful wife,
And honeft labor fanctified their life ;
Inur'd by practice to the paths of right,
No wars alarm them, and no foes affright.
But now let war or peace their influence fhed,
With hydra-fury lux'ry rears her head :
Avenger of the world the demon flies,
And troops of evils frown before our eyes.

Since

Since to French arts we've op'd the willing door,
Like France our thoughts are high, our purfes poor.

Each crime repel then to its native plain :
To Holland knav'ry, infolence to Spain ;
Let eunuch-foftnefs to Italia pafs ;
Give France her trinkets; Germany her glafs :
Ne'er, ne'er be England made from Englifh hearts
A paltry magazine of foreign arts.

So fondly females fly at pleafure's call,
They ev'n adore that fing-fong fair Vauxhall :
That foil enchanted, where all orders meet;
The gay to laugh, the citizen to eat,
And quaff his port ; while thro' his lordfhip's vein
Steals that deluder of the heart Champagne.
The mob a mind prepar'd for riot bring ;
No need to raife it by an *Indian King*.

In vain the hufbands, when their conforts roam,
The friends affemble to amufe at home ;
Thofe very friends, unlefs 'tis term'd a rout,
Grow fick of chit-chat, and ALL ramble out.
ALL, high or low, the fond affection bear ;
The landau gaping, or the one-horfe chair,
Full as the coach-and-fix the genius fuit ;
Ev'n fome, like Methodifts, will trudge on foot.

The

The flaunting widow, tho' from nothing fprung,
At cards and playhoufe triumphs, like the young ;
With Maid of Honor grac'd fhe fhines difplay'd,
Each part of drefs in fitteft order laid.
Tho' rich in gold, fhe wifely finks her plate,
Becaufe fhe will not bear a tax of ftate :
Salts, kettle, knives, and fideboard, fly away,
All but the fpoons, and thofe efcape the PAY.
The Jacobite, politically poor,
Now greets the gay affembly to her door ;
She weighs their merit from imparted mirth,
And crowns with vanities the want of birth.
The time may come when, like the ruder fex,
Well fhe may fear left poverty perplex ;
May know, too fondly if her wealth fhe ufe,
Purfes re-fill not, like the fcriptur'd cruife.
Check then thy whims, left fickle fortune turn,
And leave thee George-ftreet, and thyfelf to mourn.

If mufic fires her, the delighted fair
Will rummage Ofwald's with fantaftic care ;
And while great Handel's in the corner plac'd,
Purchafe Arne's fripperies to fhew her tafte ;
Or, if fhe ftill more modifhly would die,
A fet of Glaffes will from Schuman buy.

The Bride with treafures flufh'd, of manners rare,
Th' Italian fofters with indulgent care :

When

When fhines the treat, 'tis with her fav'rite grac'd,
At cards or table with the greateft plac'd.
Talk you of fkill, tafte, mufic, 'tis in vain,
She only liftens to Giardini's ftrain.
Eafy her lord; and reftiff when her fon,
She cries, " My concerts, if you like not, fhun."
Then bids fome maiden of her fet advance,
And, lo ! the fidler ftanding up to dance:
Nay more—the ruftics with this friend to greet,
She kindly takes him to her country-feat.
Such folly's whims, and fuch the wealthy pleafe :—
Joy to the victims of fantaftic eafe !

Are play'rs the theme ? the fair refigns her heart
To Barry ; Barry plays the lover's part:
Garrick in fuch muft furely give offence,
Too fmall a thing for parts of confequence.
Are politics the talk ? from day to day
Thrid the dull jingle of the dulleft play.
But touch not there ; unknowing how to yield
She guides the council, and commands the field :
Points the flow fchemes of France, the German rout—
Intrigues of all forts fhe at will finds out.

By foes furrounded in the dreadful ftrife
She kindly fhudders for poor Frederic's life :
(While the world's goffip fneers her wonder move,
That fuch an Hero is not form'd for love)

Difplays

Diſplays each ſecret wheel that turns the court,
Improving paſſport to each wild report,
Such at the frown of hoſtil France can lead
The deſolating ſtream o'er Holland's mead ;
Can laugh at Spaniards threat'ning Liſbon's coaſt ;
Then hint how eaſy Newfoundland was loſt.

But mark, where pride bids harmóny to ceaſe,
And, when her own is broke, breaks others' peace:
Where, ſoil'd the floor, or diſhes ill-diſplay'd,
She'll flounce, and hurl her ſlipper at the maid.
With accents foul her huſband's name ſhe brands,
And leaves the ſervant in the ſurgeon's hands.
If ſome diſſembled pain demand her care,
She's reſtleſs 'till ſhe breathes the Tunbridge-air ;
There bathes ; and boaſting of her want of wits,
The conj'rer ſeeks, who throws her into fits.
Mean while the gueſts, invited by her lord,
Sharp-ſet from Juſtice meet an empty board :
SHE by herſelf from whim inur'd to dine,
Crowns ev'ry mouthful with a ſup of wine ;
Then cyder's ſtreams, when cholics torture, roll ;
Laſt Ceres' windy draughts furcharge her foul.
Ere this, at noon (ſo modiſh paſs her days)
A cup of chocolate her ſtomach ſtays.
No wonder now, ſucceſs attends her pains,
And vex'd with ſickneſs, ſhe at length complains :

When

When lo! from fide to fide her careful friends
Strong cordials fetch; fhe drinks, and fomewhat mends.
Hail, bridegroom! happy in thy choice of life,
Whofe fondnefs truckles to fo fweet a wife!
(Prim council, fmirking with extended chin,
Soft honey all without, but gall within;
Whofe chatter'd phrafes unimpaffion'd move,
And a tame prattler of felf-int'reft prove)—
Yet, fuch, fuch only is to meannefs due,
Whofe rancor fpatters worth he never knew.

Peace to the maid, who founds with rapt'rous tongue
The midnight ftrains of meditative Young,
Yet fondly poring with a full delight,
Hangs o'er the ravings of th' Arabian Night.
Yield, authors, critics, yield; with awful ear
Bow the rich beauties of her thoughts to hear;
Still unrefifted fwell the echoing found,
Whofe loud alarum never needs be wound.
Refign, oh, man! the tube's exploring cares;
'Tis hers to regulate the moon and ftars.
Proud ethics' fons, to her fuperior light
Refign the deep refearch of good and right.
Refign, ye bards, Parnaffus' flow'ry feat,
An height reach'd only by her daring feet.

In peace, ye pow'rs, may Thyrfis' moments glide,
Free from the clamors of a learned bride,

W

Who throws around her fyllogiftic rage,
Or deals worn anecdotes from hift'ry's page;
For ever rambling with impatient tongue,
All knowledge fhe, and never in the wrong.

But chief the foliy, when her ftrains impart
Th' affected pageant of each term of art:
Each fentence ftrain'd with apteft words to fit,
She boafts to emulate the fire of Pitt.
With explanation does ftill more perplex;
Then weeps the wretched ign'rance of her fex.
Her lord's fad folecifms her rage purfues,
Her own from friendfhip ready to excufe;
Of drefs to others fhe refigns the care,
Who will, th' inhofpitable load may bear:
She views the trifles with a pitying fight,
For fuch alone inferior minds delight.

But lo! each morning, with encrufted grace,
The crack'd enamel ftands upon her face,
Abhorrent of the lip, whofe eager kifs
Shrinks from the cold, unanimated blifs.
When, fmiling in the circle of her friends,
Each dear-bought lux'ry on her nod attends;
Then her warm cheek with fofteft purple glows,
Wak'd into life each charm redoubled fhews.
Seeks fhe the country; handed by her maid,
This artificial health's to view difplay'd;

Ev'n

Ev'n for the city she must this produce,
For paint, like friends, grows needful from its use.

What then this pasted, birdlim'd being name,
This thing for ever chang'd, yet still the same ?
Her face at best but a mercurial wall,
Whose looks betray a moving hospital.

Faithful improver of his lordship's storms,
Lo ! the deep frown-my lady's face deforms ;
First of her cast-offs Abigail she cheats;
Which haste indignant to the next she meets ;
She fumes, she roars, and when fatigu'd a nod
Commands her gentleman to lift the rod ;
Next vaults into her chair ; the doubled weight
Doubles the chairmens' misery, and hate;
Then home returning, with her patch and paint
She smiles upon her guests, a perfect saint;
Turns o'er the richest silks with curious eye,
Silks, which tho' sent for, she ne'er means to buy.
Counts all her husband's faults, which strait he hears,
No need of conscience thund'ring in his ears.

Thrice happy Spaniards, whose imperious sway
Will make the proudest of the sex obey !
Bless'd, in whose mansions if the female seek
To add fresh lustre to her dress, or cheek,

G

When

When to the play her friends expectant call,
To heavy whift, or more enliven'd ball;
Tho' rough her drefs, her charms unvary'd roam ;—
Perhaps the nod commands her ftay at home.
Not hers to fret, with giddy rage betray'd,
Or, when her clothes fit ill, alarm the maid :
" Not fhe in fault," the don unruly cries,
" Your glafs will tell you where the error lies."

Not hers the licence to another's care
To leave the nice decorum of the hair ;
No mutt'ring aunt, whofe fhrivel'd hand difplays
The ill-bred induftry of ancient days ;
(Some maid with mellow'd charms of threefcore years,
Who in the trappings of nineteen appears)
Dares recommend her with intruding tongue
The vaunted modes, which rul'd when fhe was young ;
Modes, which corrected virgins in their prime
Took from herfelf to fuit them to the time.
Such was the Tow'r, whofe formidable glare
Like a huge pharos ftood fublime in air ;
A ftructure for a feafon doom'd to ftand,
Tho' built by fafhion on a moving fand.
You'd fwear, fo very tall the looks before,
'Twas fome vaft giant from th'Italian fhore ;
See her behind, and with diminifh'd grace
She finks a fifter of the pigmy race ;

Lefs

Lefs than his little lordfhip to the view;
Not, like him, lifted on a high-heel'd fhoe:

From large expences, negligence, and ftrife;
Moft find a wretched neighbor in a wife,
The wife in this alone ; her hate extends
To plague himfelf, his fervants, and his friends.
View her account-book, which donations boafts
To tricking conj'rers, methodifts, and ghofts ;
Where W—tf—ld fhines fupreme among her friends,
Prince of extortion, father of the fiends ;
Behind, ufurpers of religion's veil,
A ranting crew of brothers ftands confefs'd ;
Drums, trumpets fink before the noify PACK,
Who learn from him the founding-board to crack *.
Thefe rob you at a ftroke of heav'nly grace,
Unlefs your mite you in the moufe-trap place ;
To frenzy firing with fanatic zeal
Your very garment from your back they fteal ;
Then fwearing, you may fin fecure of harm,
Give you the cloak of faith to keep you warm.

Now wading thro' the vault's nocturnal gloom
The countefs feeks diverfion from the tomb ;
There, at each ftep, with doubts and fears o'erfpread,
For a poor childifh ghoft difturbs the dead;

* See Mr. Hogarth's expreffive print of credulity, fanaticifm, and fu-
perftition.

She

She gropes, and summons Fanny in the dark,
Fanny, that gilded play-thing to the clerk.

   Now to the conj'rer's : At his dread command
At once she's whirl'd into a foreign land ;
She quaffs the Nile, the Danube, or the Tweed,
That bathes the kingdoms, which the conj'rer breed :
His art on whiten'd walls her Sires will shew,
Feeding their sheep scarce thirty years ago.
He stamps his magic foot, and awful nods :
She hears the voice of angels and of gods.
How justly vaunts he his superior ray,
Who spreads o'er Heav'n and earth his sov'reign sway !
Whom male and female court, and youth and age,
'Theme fit for Hogarth's smile, or Brown's fantastic rage ;
The blund'ring struggles of whose motley wit
Himself professes not compos'd, but WRIT.

   This pastime over, farther to amuse
Approach the fawning fortune-telling Jews ;
From place to place these out-cast Hebrews roam,
And steal from frauds a comfortable home ;
Wisely, as Warburton, of Moses write,
And vaunt, like him, from Heav'n a clearer light.
Rewards, but less than Whitfield's, crown their schemes,
Tho' both alike retailing empty dreams.

   Behold him pointing to the simp'ring fair
Her swain, the dying father to the heir ;

Such,

Such, like the Indian, with the greateſt eaſe
Can fix the vital period as they pleaſe,
Sure as the conj'rer can of three make five,
Or headleſs chickens can reſtore alive ;
With eating ribbons, gold, nay fire, ſurprize,
And make to art a convert of the eyes.

Undoubted conqueſt, when the crew relate
How long a miniſter ſhall rule a ſtate ;
Theirs the deep ſecrets of the pow'rs above ;
The ſtateſman ſmiling in his ſov'reign's love
No longer triumphs, than by him upheld,
But ſinks, like patriots whom his arts expell'd ;
There Holles' life, in loyal buſtle ſpun,
Beams virtue's ſplendors from a ſetting ſun :
Say then, ye prophets, ſay, when wars ſhall ceaſe,
And England ſmile in honorable peace.

Joy to the happy trade, whoſe daring tale
Survives the ſtocks, the whipping-poſt, and jail ;
For fortune's ſmiles, ſome penſioners confeſs,
Not always conj'rer-politicians bleſs :
Thus vainly KINDRED mathematics ſhew,
(The truth, O ſcientific Cambridge ! know)
Unleſs the ſtorm and ſhipwreck they can boaſt,
When ſearching for the Bridge * the foreign coaſt.

From

---

* There is a propoſition in Euclid diſtinguiſhed by the name of the
" Pons Aſinorum," which the young philoſopher muſt paſs before he can

aſpire

From such the gaping son's impatient breath
Pants for the period of his mother's death ;
To fix his uncle's fate the Wager tries,
Sure to gain something, if he lives or dies.
The flutt'ring maidens, anxious for their swains,
Aſk o'er their love what awful planet reigns';
When the fond ſtars will ſhed their genial light,
The nuptial ſtars, which happy ſouls unite.

    Nor more to union ſuited is the wife,
Who from the weather-glaſs conducts her life ;
Who hugs the ſiſter-changeling to her breaſt,
From ills, her fancy propheſies, unbleſs'd.
No need for health the faculty to bribe,
Unerring Almanacs the path preſcribe ;
Ne'er with her huſband ſeen ; the reaſon's known ;
Her author tells her to go out alone ;
This ſhe retracts, her carriage at the door,
Becauſe a cat has croſs'd her on the floor ;
Now 'gainſt her neighbor dreads ſome fatal ſtroke,
Becauſe pies chatter, or a glaſs is broke.
When ſick her ſtomach, or inflam'd her eye,
One ſtated hour muſt remedies apply ;

aſp're to the hopes of becoming a profound mathematician. The more
experienced ſtudents have in their turn a Bridge, which it may be feared
no one will ever be able to paſs ; viz. The longitude.

If

If low her ftation, for a trivial gain
Some wand'ring Gipfy will her fate explain;
Rul'd by the proffer'd fee, whofe mighty fkill
With good exalts her, or dejects with ill.

Mean while the wealthy, from the mode of town;
The city feek for conj'rers of renown;
(That bufy foil, with richeft fenfe replete,
Where all from wealth are conj'rers whom you meet)
Who boaft no deeper meaning by their tricks,
Than court-divines who talk of politics.
The buxom houfemaid, tripping thro' the ftreets,
At fome church-porch the mutt'ring grandame meets;
She opes her hand, and points her future life,
When John the butler's, or the coachman's wife;
" No fortune's frown fhall quafh the nuptial joy,
" She'll crown thy wifhes with a blooming boy."
Then bids her for a moon her health beware,
Nor rufh like fome, untimely to the air.
So flows the nonfenfe; and to crown the whole
She iffues Powders for a wand'ring foul.
Say, giddy wretch, can witchcraft's cheats impart
Recover'd fondnefs to a hufband's heart?
But go,—too foon with fondling arts beguil'd,
Go,—of the parent rob the tender child;

G 4

Go,

Go, rob thyfelf; and then convicted read,
How oft to death alone the med'cines lead *.

Lo! the poor foundling of fome wealthy maid
Smiles in the foft'ring hofpital difplay'd;
The prieft, as prophet of his future fame,
Gives it a peer's, perhaps the father's name.
Hail, happy fhoots! by Heav'n's indulgent care
Refign'd to charity's ferener air;
Let giddy worldlings, of unfeeling breaft,
Brand her mild influence with a pointlefs jeft,
By her to worth, religion, valor grown,
Some lords might wifh the offspring for their own.

See Ruffia's fiend, at priefthood's mad control,
Shakes in the hero's garb her emp'ror's foul:
One hand the dagger, one the paper bears,
To force him headlong from the kingdom's cares.
And why?—" His foul too narrow for a crown,
" He finks a bigot to a king's renown †."
Sound reafon this the poifon'd drug t' infufe,
Then fpread a timely cholic in the news!

---

* The original thought is here varied; the reafon, on comparifon, is obvious. In the imitation a fubject is treated, which, however trivial it may at firft fight appear, has been too often rendered ferious from its confequences.

† King of Pruffia. The ftrongeft plea that has been urged for the fa-vage action.

And

And is it thus religion greets the fight?
Thus leaps infatiate o'er the bounds of right?
While thirfty priefts, inhuman in their will,
Like women-thieves from daftard fpirits kill.

   Seek you the murd'rer of a private name?
Mark unrelenting Blandy's favage flame;
That flame which finks her father to the grave,
Whom nature could but for a feafon fave:
Far bafer fhe, who 'gainft a nation's fire
Could animate a mob's rebellious fire.
But fay, did jealous hatred urge the blow?—
His only offspring perith'd long ago;
Or glow'd thy foul impatient, on the throne
To rear fome prince, fome baftard of thy own?
How vain the caution with a fparing lip
The proffer'd treafures of the feaft to fip!
Flown is each friend; the tyrant's hands afford
No faving Tafter to a captive's board.

   'Tis true, the Ruffian's unrelenting rage
May found a novel to a future age;
The mufe on fancy's aid may feem to call,
Juft as the frothy jargon of Fingal;
Whom dotards father on the Galic ftrain,
Tho' the meer rattle of Macpherfon's brain.

Refent-

Refentment's guilt (thank Heav'n!) we only view
In meaner mortals, and th' examples few;
Thefe ftragling fhew in indolence's book *
Or the bruis'd houfemaid, or the mangled cook.

Let India's wives exert their favage fkill;
Our polifh'd females teize us to their will.
No wonder then Medea's threadbare dream
Again finds matter for the tragic theme.

Sunk lie, O man! in wealth's intemp'rate love,
The fofter fex more mild affections prove;
A tranfient frown tho' fometimes we behold,
Too great the pains to be a downright fcold.
Chairs, difhes, glaffes, in confufion hurl'd,
The cares and tempefts of a buftling world,
Were made for man; they fuit the Vandal's tafte;
The fair fret only when a cap's ill-plac'd.

Yet fome there are, who coldly prim from fchool,
Void of all reafon, choofe to err by rule;
Die o'er the hift'ry where the hufband's life
Is the fole comfort of a fondling wife;
Then hug fome fav'rite lap-dog, and with fighs,
" Oh! how can Lucia live when Fiddy dies."

* The news.

Thofe

Thofe defp'rate heroines, whom our fchool-boys fe
For want of better, in the mufty Greek ;
Who when their wifhes have obtain'd a man
Get free again as early as they can,
Our fair abhor ; a diff'rent path they choofe,
Studious to gain a hufband, not to lofe.
Thrice happy they, whofe hufbands to infure
The news for each difeafe prefcribe a cure ;
Thrice happy, England, in thy favor'd fate,
Where quacks the fubject prop, and Brown the ftate.

THE

THE

SEVENTH SATIRE

IMITATED.

WHERE lives the patron of the tuneful nine,
Cheer'd by whose smile the rays of genius shine?
Scarce one, alas! can forrowing learning boaft;
The name of patron in the vain is loft.

Nor wonder infult's fervil pamphlets fpread,
Juft fcribled over for the author's bread;
No wonder dullnefs taints the hungry ftain,
While hawkers cry the labors of the brain:
'Tis yours, ye rich, to aid the gen'rous toil,
For learning thrives not on a barren foil.

Tune

Tune forth, my bard, yet think not to behold
The great man's favor, or the proffer'd gold;
Far other arts your empty cheft muft fill,—
Turn player, money-jobber,—what you will;
A fteward wealthy from entrufted ftore,
The houfe, the manor buy, thy lord's before.
Important Fop, to profe it be thy doom,
(Not on militias) in an auction-room;
To plate, goods, linen, draw furrounding looks,
O'er pictures die, and cut dull jefts on books;
While round thee mean ill-manner'd natures fhed
Difhoneft fneers of fcandal on the dead.
Full to the times each ftrain of falfhood fit;
On worth rewarded fhow'r thy wanton wit;
To footh encroaching Spain, and humbler Gaul,
Ev'n Pitt a traitor to his country call;
Laft, by mock-worfhip crown your virtues' lift,
And do rich penance in a—methodift.

Sunk are the fouls, whofe bounty could reftrain
The facred virgins to Britannia's plain;
From thefe no more the tuneful fweets they fhed,
No more the laurel rears its blooming head;
Tho' free-born Churchill wake the gen'rous fire,
True tafte alone is patron of his lyre;
While Northern fyllabubs regale the great,
Fingal—the literary feaft of ftate.

Still

Still from the world your flimfy labors hide,
Nor friendfhip urge ye to an author's pride ;
Tear, tear the offspring of an idle hour,
Let chefts conceal them, and let moths devour.
Alike in vain your felf-lov'd numbers fing
A buftling minifter, and fighting king ;
In vain ferener thoughts your ftrains employ,
Unfhaken friendfhip, or domeftic joy ;
Still may ye write, ftill fix'd your wretched doom
To live fequefter'd in a garret's gloom ;
While, tho' each coxcomb boafts your pictur'd face,
The author finds not at his board a place.

There are, 'tis true, who ftreams of praifes grant,
But grudge one piece, tho' confcious of your want.
The ftrain delights them (fo complete their tafte)
When with the trappings of the binder grac'd :
(As on my lord the fondling fpaniels gloat
Each virtue center'd in th' embroider'd coat)
Thus trifling on, ye tune the fofter lays,
And idly fpend the vigor of your days,
The days beft fuited to feverer care,
To ocean's labors, and the ftorms of war ;
Laft, crufh'd by age, in poverty ye pine,
And fighing curfe the unavailing nine.

Yet fir'd by wealth, your fteps with fond refort
For grandeur leave your own Apollo's court ;

To
3

To fuch ye pour the incenfe of the line,
Which calls a booby fage, a wretch divine.
Or fhould grim priefthood fwell the daring thought,
How glows the page with facred wifdom fraught!
Let Pope and Shakefpear point HIS judgment's care,
Tho' flung by Edwards from the critic's chair;
While NEW-COIN'D truth his lab'ring genius fits,
The great coloffus o'er the race of wits;
Whofe ftreams of Learning deign'd anon to fchool
Intemp'rate Wefley, felf-convicted fool!

Thus Ford by flatt'ry rais'd, diftinguifh'd name!
With notes fantaftic courts th' applaufe of fame.
Each crouded box the fons of lux'ry grace,
Nought there confpicuous, but a noble's face.
From thefe th' unfkilful peals of praife refound,
But few, few critics deck the gall'ry's round.
A fober tribe, who friends to folid fenfe,
Were ne'er fufficient for the night's expence,
She ftarts, fhe fhrieks, the ranks fo thinly plac'd,
And wonders at her country's want of tafte.

Yes, genius droops; the world with fond regard
For half-form'd libels quit the facred bard;
While worthlefs priefthood, with unhallow'd hands,
(So fafhion, man's delufive fiend, commands)
The hireling echo of fome flave of ftate,
Spits motley flander on the truly great.

Far

Far hence be fuch; the poet's ample vein,
Whofe foaring fancy pours th' immortal ftrain;
Wrap'd in whofe page the full-blown graces roll,
Catch the warm bofom, and enflame the foul,
Springs boldly forth thro' wit's untrodden ways,
Nor vulgar drofs deforms his fterling lays.
'Tis his a ftranger to intruding care,
No ills to torture, and no frowns to fcare,
In calm contentment's peaceful vale to roam,
Eafe his attendant, and each fhade his home:
Mute elfe the lyre, no verdant laurels grow,
Chill'd by the blaft of poverty and woe.

Encircling pleafures Prior's page improve,
And add frefh beauties to the fweets of love;
For Henry's vows, and Emma's heav'nly fmile,
He quits the pangs of minifterial toil;
The mufe, controling like the charming fair,
Calls from each other thought the bofom's care.

See highly feated in the realms of fame
Great Milton fhines; whofe ftrains with glowing flame
Fair order's fmile o'er chaos' wafte difplay,
And pour on ancient night the beams of day;
Paint the fell fiends from heav'nly tranfports hurl'd,
And fin firft frowning o'er a new-born world;
Oh! had religion crown'd thy gen'rous plan,
And what adorn'd the poet grac'd the man;

H   Had'ft

Had'ſt thou not ſervil rear'd rebellion's rod,
Deluded penſioner of Cromwell's nod,
How wert thou bleſs'd ! but now with pitying eyes
We view the author, while the work we prize.
Yes, we deſpiſe the man whoſe tragic rage
Crowns with all Athens' ſtores an Engliſh ſtage ;
Tunes warm'd to ire, and ſoften'd into ſport
A madden'd Sampſon, and a joyous court.

    See Wilmot, fav'rite of a careleſs reign,
To love and rapture gives th' immodeſt ſtrain.
For him fair friendſhip boaſts no winning charms,
Each thought reſigning in a harlot's arms ;
Gay ſcenes of lux'ry rule his ſoften'd ſenſe,
The dupe of folly, riot, and expence.
Sleep on, degen'rate, wrap'd in midnight gloom,
But know, diſgrace ſtill waits thee in the tomb :
An erring Dryden claims our conſcious ſighs,
But Wilmot's crimes hang frowning to the eyes.

    Inſpir'd by Dryden's animated page,
What crowding numbers ſeek the proſp'ring ſtage !
With peals of joy they plead the poet's cauſe,
And ſhake the gall'ries with their loud applauſe.
Yet ſcarce from works the needy bard could live,
Thro' which the pamper'd play'rs triumphant thrive.
Thus nobly form'd each heav'nly theme to fit,
He ſunk to ſtews his proſtituted wit ;

While

While varying glows the particolor'd page,
With truth's bright ſtores, and irreligion's rage :
View, view, ye bards, nor flatter ſlaves of ſtate,
No treaſures bleſs ye from the rich and great ;
No merit from the ſoil of grandeur ſprings,
Which flatt'ry plants with ribbons and with ſtrings.

Envy begone, nor read with jealous looks
The tuneful labors of the poet's books ;
Tho' Lanſdowne once with ſweeteſt ſmile could ſhine,
Fav'rite alike, and patron of the nine ;
With gallant jeſt tho' Stanhope's lively wit
To poliſh'd courts the ſatire's ſting could fit ;
To needy genius tend the proffer'd gold,
Yet Lanſdowne's dead, and Cheſterfield is old :
Both cent'ring now in one diſtinguiſh'd name,
Reſign to Lyttelton the poſt of fame.

From ſuch ere while the bard with ardent ſoul
Bad in full nerve the ſacred numbers roll ;
Th' hiſtorian fir'd with learning's ceaſeleſs rage
In midnight-ſtudies plann'd the labor'd page ;
Sheets urg'd on ſheets in goodly mountains riſe,
And feaſt with ancient ſtores th' admiring eyes.
But now no patrons ope the gates of fame,
Lux'ry has long repreſs'd the gen'rous flame ;
All ſpurn the raptures of the rhyming throng,
Saunt'rers the bards, and numbers but a ſong ;

H 2
And

And hift'ry's charms in living luftre bloom
But from the pens of Robertfon and Hume.

Survey the troops which fill the wrangling bar,
What written labors form the golden war !
Whence fprings th' unruly heat, th' unpolifh'd cry,
To face down truth, and varnifh out a lye ?
Or, deck'd with innocency's fofteft fmile,
Each word, each look difplays a friendly toil ?
Whence?—but that clients with an anxious fire
Gaze on each look, and ev'ry word infpire.
While worn-out warriors in a mournful lift
Scarce on their country's fcanty pay fubfift,
The infants' cry, the murmurs of th' opprefs'd,
Of injur'd freedom, and of worth diftrefs'd,
Sigh forth to thefe ; to thefe exhale the ftrain,
Tho' pride and dullnefs rule the judge's brain.
Go then, thou fhatter'd victor of the caufe,
Go, boaft the juftice of thy country's laws ;
The cofts defray ; then, voice of truth, proclaim,
Thou art in nought the conq'ror, but the name.

What folid hopes the pleader's ardor move,
Let Scotia's quick-difcerning offspring prove ;
Of old the flow'ry Tully of the bar,
Now high-exalted in the gilded car :
The haughty tyrant, as he moves along,
Looks down imperious on the abject throng,

As

As form'd by nature of too mean a clay
To fhare with him the fplendors of the day.
Yet fome unknowing of the voice of praife
No pains can profit, and no labors raife ;
Still doom'd to talk, ftill fated to be curs'd
In the low ftate where fortune plac'd them firft.
While Mutius fwelling with applaufe and gain
Sees num'rous vaffals form his crowded train.
Yet not the veftment's pride, the title's glow
The plenteous acres, and the villa's fhew,
From confcious fcorn th' uplifted heart defend,
Whofe actions frown unworthy of a friend.

The lavifh people, with a fond regard,
Show'r on the fons of law the great reward ;
Yet ere they proffer, fafhion guides the breaft—
To judge the wealthieft pleader for the beft ;
To fix your worth, and ftamp the full-blown pride,
Ye lawyers, like phyficians, firft muft ride.
The formal pageant of a fenfelefs prig
Confirms the virtues of a rev'rend wig ;
O'er needy eloquence while infults fpread ;
The poor in pocket are alike in head.

Go, rather buftle 'mid the cannons' roar,
Fly to the loud alarms of India's fhore :
There, great oppofer of the troops of Gaul,
There bravely conquer, or as bravely fall ;

Thus

Thus, like undaunted Wolfe, thy gen'rous toils
Shall meet the full reward,—in England's fmiles.

Survey the realms of learning's facred feat,
And mark the manners of the fam'd retreat:
The ftripling, fir'd the fecret fprings to know
Whence myftic nature's various caufes flow,
(Where the dull foe of genius brighteft fhines
Thro' the ftern midnight of pedantic lines)
With rage redoubled fills the ftudious plan,
And drops the child to emulate the man.
Say, fhould he toil with unavailing will,
Curs'd with a plodding tutor's bufy fkill,
Glares not inftruction with the want of wit?
When diff'rent themes the fcholar beft would fit.

Go, lively youth, with happier ardor pour
The polifh'd declamation's claffic fhow'r;
Point out the patriot's toil, the hero's fcar,
The fhouting fquadrons, and tumultuous war:
Friend to thy genius, an enraptur'd fire
Will praife the labors, and reward the fire.
With fons of learning wage the vig'rous ftrife,
'Twill fhed kind influence on thy future life;
'Twill bid thy cheek with doubled fury glow,   •
'Mid the full fenate to confront a foe;
From virtue's breaft to ward oppreffion's dart,
And blaft each purport of the guilty heart;

                                          Such

Such manly rage the rich return will yield,
Adorn the bar, or confecrate the field.

How fmall the backward fire's expence and joy,
To form the manners of the tender boy !
Coop'd up the victim of fome pedant fool,
He's ftamp'd a booby—at the cheapeft fchool.
Mean while the prancing fteeds in aukward ftate
Sport with gay trappings at HIS crouded gate;
Superior neatnefs points the vaffal's care,
Becaufe a wealthy knave would take the air.
Rear'd by his giddy nod the columns rife,
Which feem to look defiance to the fkies ;
Within each lux'ry, glorious to behold,
Beams forth of painting, marble, and of gold;
Treats which would feed a Quin's infatiate fmell,
No Englifh cook could POISON half fo well.
Thus fhines his childrens' foe, th' unworthy's friend,
Who grudges only where he moft fhould fpend.

But whence does Clodio crown'd with treafures glow,
(Such happy lot th' inferior rarely know)
Cheer'd with the fplendors of preferment's hour,
And fam'd at once for wifdom, birth, and pow'r ?
Fix'd to his own, tho' deaf to Britain's good,
Each change of court this ductil merc'ry ftood :
Now glutted av'rice checks the flumb'ring tongue,
Refigning rules and motions to the young.

H 4

The

The genial ſtar, which crowns the natal day,
Diſplays o'er future ſcenes its ſacred ray ;
Thus from the humbler ſubjeƈt's ruſtic fate
Was Cromwell lifted to the throne of ſtate :
And oft the vulgar grandeur's tools are made,
Who ſprang from parents of mechanic trade.
True noble HE who ſpurns corruption's hour,
And mocks the ſtorms of miniſterial pow'r ;
That pow'r which ſpeaks (bold ſatire !) to his face,
" Go rev'rence wealth and virtue in his grace."
Th' undaunted Patriot, ,fan'd by gen'rous fires,
Repeats his vig'rous counſel, and RETIRES.

Lie, ſacred grandſires, wrap'd in peaceful reſt ;
Thou, gentle earth, ſink lightly on their breaſt ;
Each breathing ſweetneſs ſhow'r its charms around,
And ſpring eternal deck the hallow'd ground ;
You bad the ſtripling glow with wiſdom's fire,
And the pure teacher ſtamp the gen'rous fire.
Not yours the voice to trill the ſoften'd ſong,
Or ſhed the nonfenſe of a witleſs tongue ;
Fair wiſdom's ſtrains ſtill warbled in your ear,
Strains which our modiſh ſons would laugh to hear ;
Would ſpurn th' inſtruƈtor's lore at pleaſure's call,
And ſwear his knowledge of the world was ſmall.

What taunts of dullneſs damp the teacher's breaſt,
His learning hated, and himſelf a jeſt !

The

The liv'ry'd minions catch th' inhuman ſtrain;
Ev'n my young MASTER liſps with parrot vein.
Yield, chaplain, yield, the rude deriſion bear,
At beſt thou upper-ſervant to a peer;
Expeſtant ſtill, when clos'd the ſcene of ſtrife,
Of ſome ſmall Living for tny eve of life.
For this inſpir'd by learning's hireling rage
Thou keep'ſt long vigils o'er the ſacred page;
Ploughing with anxious toil a ſtubborn plain
To ſuit pure reaſon to a booby's brain;
For this ſtill poring 'mid th' incumbent gloom,
The lifeleſs lamp juſt winking o'er the room,
While Locke frowns black with many a ſoiling ſpot,
And Clarke's foul'd margin labors with the blot.

Ye friends of learning's venerable cauſe,
Diſplay to youth the ſalutary laws;
Bid them ſagacious glean from hiſt'ry's page
The moral diſtates of each diſtant age.
Let others ſeek, on trifling themes intent,
A cit's huge line, or RECENT peer's deſcent;
Let others ſkill'd in faſhion's follies ſhew
The jewel'd matron, or the whiſp'ring beau;
Or, fir'd by heraldry's fantaſtic charms,
Point out each brother blockhead—by his Arms.
Be yours to fix with truth's perſuaſive art
In honor's nobler paths the ſtripling's heart.

Youth,

Youth, soft as wax, with virtue's stamp imprefs'd,
Still keeps the picture imag'd on its breast;
The polish'd gay may form with softer grace
The pictur'd landscape, and the virgin's face ;
Be yours the prize to loftier scenes resign'd,—
Their skill the taste improve, but yours the mind.

T H E

THE

EIGHTH SATIRE

IMITATED.

YES, yes—the charms of grandeur all are vain;—
The board rich-fmoaking, and the hireling train,
The gilded car, the canopy of ftate,
Are but the fhining trifles of the great;
Unlefs to clofe the fpecious fcene we find
Fair honor's feal full-ftamp'd upon the mind.

What means the gallery's fpacious length to fhew
Paternal faces in refplendent row;
What means the time-worn, venerable buft,
Or ftatue clouded with religious ruft,
Which full to view the valued grin difclofe,
A broken fhoulder, or a fhatter'd nofe?

What

What boots, that grandeur's voice triumphant cry
" Lo! here the father of my family;
" And here my grandfire, that diftinguifh'd lord,
" By nations honor'd, and by kings ador'd?"
When after all the boaft we view within
The dupe of folly, and the flave of fin.

   Say, if the warrior, whofe undaunted force
Is call'd to quafh the foe's impetuous courfe,
If he, enchain'd by ev'ry modifh vice,
With flippant finger fhake the founding dice;
And wafte in play thofe moments of the night,
Of old he fpent amid the toils of fight;
Alas! how finks he 'mongft the great enrol'd,
Whofe worth is title, and whofe virtue gold?

   Is there who dares not ev'n his finger bare,
Should Zephyr wave a ruder breath of air;
Who fteps, clofe cover'd from the folar ray,
Left his fair face fhould fuffer by the day?
Is there, in whofe degen'rate foul we trace
No deed but ferves to vilify his race;
Who, bafely cloak'd in friendfhip's fair difguife,
Show'rs o'er his neighbor fcandal's blackeft lies?—
From grandeur's lift the foul pretender blot;
Be his the coward's and the villain's lot.

Shew

Shew me the man, whose conscience truly just
Beams uncorrupt in honor's sacred trust ;
Nor tow'ring on the privilege of birth,
Whose words are goodness, and whose deeds are worth ;
Him grandeur's darling son my soul can spy
Thro' the deep gloom of unknown anceftry ;
Yes—I survey him ; hail, diftinguifh'd great !
To thee fair virtue gives the chair of ftate ;
To thee the general and the ftatesman yield,
The chief alike in council and the field ;
Surrounding thousands conscious joy difplay,
And fhouts triumphant lead thee in thy way.
Ye flaves of title, grandeur's baftard race,
Here reverence honor—and give virtue place ;
Low bow, and ftamp this truth upon your breaft,
That " grandeur is but worth with fplendor drefs'd."

As well fome giant might the voice of mirth
Call pooreft pigmy of the fons of earth ;
As well o'er beauty might a Paris yield
To fome crook'd dwarf the triumph of the field ;
As blacken'd o'er with fpotted crimes proclaim
An empty title in the roll of fame.
Go then, thou fool, th' unwieldy groveling fwine
Match with the courfer of diftinguifh'd line ;
Go, while he rolls bemir'd with filth and mud,
Call him the king, the lion of the wood ;

Then

Then fay, that grandeur fhining thro' the ftar
Is virtue's fplendor blazing from afar ;
Virtue, which elfe would unlamented lie,
To live difhonor'd, and in defarts dye.—

But lo! enrag'd exclaims fome flave of ftate,
WHOSE actions claim this picture of the great?
Whofe, but thine own?—the ftrokes, Lorenzo, fee,
Confefs the likenefs, it was made for thee.
Why rais'd aloft on Grandeur's blazing tow'r,
Why gafps thy bofom in the beams of pow'r?
When not one virtue decks thy tainted mind,
To mark thee from the refufe of mankind.
Befide—thy birth what ENVY'D honors grace?
Caft but an eye, vain upftart, on thy race ;
See! to what dregs thou ow'ft thy vaunted life,
Sprung from fome failor's trull, or foldier's wife.
Hence, hence the boafts of venerable birth ;
Whom call'ft thou, tyrant, nothings of the earth?
Know, thofe to infamy thy fcorn wou'd thruft,
Who dare to tell their lineage, and be juft ;
Whofe actions deck the parents whence they fprung ;
Be gone—and check the licence of thy tongue.

Th' inferior poor diftinguifh'd virtues raife,
And break the clouds of birth with dazzling blaze,
There are, who bulwarks of the nation's laws,
Defend an upftart blockhead's finking caufe ;

Thrid

Thrid ev'ry quirk, unravel ev'ry knot,
Nor breathe like thee, to die and be forgot.
Behold the * Chief, o'er diftant feas who flew
To ftill the tumults of a boift'rous crew,
And rufhing fearlefs of the war's alarms,
Bad Gallia dread the thunder of the arms;
(Deeds o'er the world whofe blazing fplendors fhone,
But ill requited by the faithlefs throne :)
Such, fuch are they—(O blufh with confcious fhame!)
Who, climbing high each fteep of glory, claim
The poft of grandeur, and the wreath of fame.

Come then, fantaftic wretch, thy bofom cloy.
With all the dainties of luxurious joy;
Fill high the treafures of the foaming bowl,
And fatiate all the wifhes of thy foul;
Drown ev'ry fenfe, nor give thine eye to fee,
What others are, and what thyfelf fhould'ft be.

Turn, haughty grandeur, turn thee to the courfe;
There view the triumphs of the gen'rous horfe;
Whofe feet victorious, rivals of the wind,
Prefs on the goal, and leave the foe behind;
Mark but his print the foremoft of the duft,
Then own to fame his title—to be juft.
Not from victorious fires his worth he claims,
Or the long lineage of a thoufand names;

* Q. Anne's Duke of Marlborough.

Not

(The heraldry of Peers outvying far,
Infur'd to life by Heber's calendar)
Not others' toil fuperior pride beftows,
'Tis to himfelf alone the prize he owes.
Not fo the fteed, whofe flow-pac'd fteps difgrace
The well-fought conquefts of his ancient race ;
'Tis his in dark oblivion's gloom to mourn
Contempt of courfers, and the mafter's fcorn ;
Of flavifh toil the meaneft poft to fill,
To drag a plough-fhare, or to turn a mill.
Thus fhould thy foul triumphant glories claim
From the mere fplendors of a father's name,
Know, 'tis intrinfic worth the man difplays,
His vices cenfure, as his virtues praife.

Away; no more in borrow'd luftre fhine ;
Nor truft the elm's embrace, thou feeble vine ;
The ftrong-built ftructure mocks the tempeft's courfe,
Supported by the pillar's pond'rous force :
Wreft but the prop, the building totters round,
And with a wafte of ruin fpreads the ground.

Dare be thyfelf ; in genuine beauties drefs'd
Let virtue fway the empire of thy breaft ;
Nor let corruption's lure thy thoughts control
To fpeak the thing, which fhocks an honeft foul.
Full in thy face tho' inquifitions frown'd,
While ev'ry fcene of torture rag'd around ;

Or

Or fome religious bigot, mad with zeal,
Low'r'd a ftern fmile, and jefting fhew'd the wheel;
Deaf to his threats with heart undaunted ftand,
And firm to virtue fpurn the dread command;
Nor fell a blifs fecure of fortune's pow'r
For the vain bleffings of a dubious hour.

For know, tho' plenty decks his fmiling board
With all the charms of fortune's treafures ftor'd;
Tho' circl'd round with ev'ry pomp of ftate,
Attendant vaffals pour into his gate;
Yet grandeur's fav'rite like the poor muft go,
Where finks ambition to difgrace and woe.

But thou, whofe wifhes at preferment's fhrine
Bid the rich flames of choiceft incenfe fhine,
At length fhould fortune for her darling gain
Some glorious embaffy to France or Spain;
Let not corruption's views thy bofom guide,
No gilded joys of vanity or pride;
With fervent voice thy country's praife proclaim,
Dwell on the triumphs of her deathlefs fame;
When captive Britons mourn, unjuftly prefs'd,
Let vengeance thunder from thy gen'rous breaft;
Go; rufh with confcious anger to their cell;
Unbind their fetters, and their cares difpel;
In vain by frowns reftrain'd, by threats withftood—
Correct the guilty, and reward the good.

I

Ne'er

Ne'er roufe with haughty fcorn a nation's hate,
But think of Villars—near the throne of ftate;
The menial vaffal of a fickle Lord
Each breathing gale fhow'r'd treafures on his board;
Crown'd with the triumph of his prince's love,
Ev'n thofe who hated dar'd not to reprove:
While mighty arbiter of peace and war
He rul'd the doom of kingdoms from afar.
Thus fmil'd his foul in grandeur's carelefs range,
But fate will fail us, and a monarch change;
Behold him now, fad fpectacle of pow'r,
He finks defpondent in misfortune's hour;
Behold him fhudd'ring with a guilty fear,
No hand to raife him, and no friend to cheer,
Hate ev'n himfelf, and curfe the fatal day,
When firft he trod ambition's fteepy way.

Say, did THAT ghaftly agonizing face
Bafk in the funfhine of a monarch's grace?
That heart, which fcarce can heave, deprefs'd with woe,
E'er beat with tranfport, or with grandeur glow?
Where droop the hands, whofe eager grafp of old
Toil'd over mountains of repeated gold?
Where finks the fmile that crown'd his dazzling ftate,
E'er fortune quafh'd him with his fovereign's hate!
This grandeur's lot, when free'd from ev'ry care
She fmiles ferene in glory's Zephyr-air;

Ere

Ere long to view the raging tempeſt riſe,
And blaſt the ſplendors of her milder ſkies.

Thine now no more the hour unknown to woe,
Doom'd to the rapine of the ſtateſman-foe;
Thine own no more the gilded palace ſtands,
Its charms fly tranſient to another's hands;
The field, the park, the ſteed, thou muſt reſign,
Yon ſingle EWE no longer to be thine;
Hence, hence—begone, the ſtateſman cries with ſcorn,
'Tis mine to triumph, but 'tis thine to mourn:—
Quit then the ſtage, no PRISONER of pow'r;
And hug the bleſſings of retirement's hour.

Chief, grandeur, chief, the dang'rous rock avoid,
The rock, which oft thy vaſſals has deſtroy'd;
Ne'er ſwell'd inebriate with preferment's reign,
Stop kind attention to thy country's pain;
Curs'd be the wretch, whoſe haughty ſteps have flown
Oppreſſion's ſteepy heights to mount a throne;
Whoſe ſoul, rapacious of th' increaſing ſtore,
Diſdains the ſorrows of the ſtarving poor;
Take, take, inſatiate fiend, their ALL away,
Graſp the rich prize, and hug the ſparkling prey;
But know, when bold deſpair awakes their eyes,
Offended courage will to vengeance riſe;
Arms ſtill are theirs; their arms inflame their ire,
While foes in tranſport rouſe the raging fire;

Arms,

Arms, arms are theirs; they pour the tempeſt round,
Ruſh to the throne, and ſtrike thee, to the ground.
Attend—the muſe no vain alarms diſplays;
'Tis truth that dictates, ane inſpires the lays.

If thou, the pillar of religious worth,
Befriend'ſt the man of honour, not of birth;
If bleſs'd with ſacred ſanctity of life,
The duteous children, and the tender wife;
Or if true patriots of undaunted zeal,
Thou liv'ſt a votary to thy country's weal;
No gaping courtiers cringing round thy door,
For ever open to the good, and poor;
Then, then alone, I'll call thee truly great,
And pour the richeſt incenſe at thy gate.
Yes, take each title that inſpires thy mind,
Thou claim'ſt thy due, thou Titus of mankind;
Heroes and patriots ſhall thy lineage grace,
Ev'n monarchs ſelves ſhall crown thy mighty race.

But if thy hands, in ſlaughter's ſtreams imbru'd,
Inceſſant riot in a looſe of blood;
If, proudly trampling on another's rights,
Ambition fires thee, or if luſt incites;
If ſtill thou revell'ſt in th' oppreſſive joys,
Till the arm wearies, and the boſom cloys;
Curſe on thy birth,—no traces I deſcry,
But of a haughty murd'rer rear'd on high;

Inſulted

Infulted lineage ftares thee in the face,
Thy nation's monfter, and thy friend's difgrace.

And know, ye tow'ring vaffals of the ftate,
Th' offence increafes as the offender's great;
Each fmalleft fpeck officious tongues difplay,
And tear ye naked to the face of day.

Ah! what avails the title's borrow'd glow,
What all the fcenes of pageanty and fhew!
Ah! what avails that honor's lifts proclaim
A grandfire's virtues to the heights of fame!
If in the fon's degenerate deeds we find
A bafe corruption taints the fervile mind;
Or if a coward foul his fears difplay,
Where the triumphant father won the day?

At once the luftre of his line to ftain,
Indignant St. John pour'd his impious ftrain;
Deaf to each dictate of religion's laws,
He tow'rs in blafphemy's detefted caufe;
And trampling full o'er virtue's facred bounds,
Scoffs at fair honor, and on reafon frowns;
'Tis true, that death the fland'rer's eyes had feal'd
E'er the fell ferpent's to the world reveal'd;
Oppofing confcience veil'd the deift's fire,
Which worthlefs frenzy could alone admire.

But

But now the raging peſt, diſplay'd to ſight,
'Treads with preſumptuous ſtep the realms of light,
With dauntleſs fury flames th' invet'rate line,
The foe alike of layman and divine ;
Still ſwells the tempeſt with a ſtern diſdain,
As truth were feeble and reſiſtance vain.

  Now arm'd with all the inſolence of ire,
Grovels the page in ſcandal's blackeſt mire ;
And opes with doubled frenzy ev'ry ſluice,
'That ſtops the ſtream of ſatire and abuſe ;
But—varying now each feature of the breaſt,
He treads the paths of humor and of jeſt ;
Whoſe treach'uous ſmiles each virtuous note would ſtill,
Were but his genius deſp'rate as his will.

  But hark ; attend the injur'd voice of ſtate ;
" Why Cenſor ſwell the vices of the great ?
" Where lives the man, in whoſe diſtinguiſh'd mind
" No lurking principle of ill we find ?"

  There are, 'tis true, whom virtue's ſtricter muſe
Their faults might pardon, and ev'n ſins excuſe :
Not ſo the wretch whoſe head-long ſtrains diſplay
An hell-born fury in the face of day ;
When ſuch the venom, ſuch the madden'd vein,
What ſon of virtue can from wrath refrain ?

                                        Behold

Behold the king * with joy-devoted foul !
Loll at his eafe, and fip the chearful bowl ;
Lull'd in the filken dream of carelefs joy,
No dangers fire him, and no pleafures cloy;
When lo ! the Gaul, with unrefifted courfe,
Sneers at the vengeance of the Britifh force:
War, war, Britannia roars with furious zeal,
To arms, to arms, exclaims the public weal:
In vain—the king reclines fecure of care,
Clafp'd in the foft embraces of the fair.
What tho' the injur'd kingdom roufe to arms,
Serene he liftens to the war's alarms ;
Surveys from far the tumults of the fhore,
And carelefs flumbers, while the cannons roar.

His gaudy court no gen'rous deeds improve,
The feat of beauty, and the throne of love ;
Severer thoughts the bufy fceptre quit,
And leave the reins to vanity and wit.
Nor formal doubts control the courtier's breaft,
All, as their king, with freedom ply the jeft ;
Spurn'd are the nation's cries, the foldiers' toils ;
What courtier forrows when a monarch fmiles !

But fay, fhould fortune's hoftil frown afford
Some thoughtlefs Charles for vaffal to thy board,

* Charles II.
I 4

Would'ft

Would'ft thou not doom th' unworthy flave in fcorn
To toil in gallies, or in jails to mourn?
Believe me, vice become not robes of ftate,
But frowns lefs dreadful in the poor than great;
The flave I view with lefs impatient eyes
Than Charles, regardlefs of a kingdom's cries.

Unhappy king! behold him prefs'd with want,
What moft his foul detefts conftrain'd to grant;
No more, as flufh'd with plenty's fmiling hour,
Hug the fweet founds of arbitrary powr;
No more in harlots' laps his wealth to fpill,
But ufe fubfervient to a nation's will:
And well—(fuch deeds their raging fouls provoke)—
This other Charles they call'd not to the block.

Not but the foul difdains the courtiers' crimes,
Slaves of ambition, vaffals to the times;
Yes, they enflame the mufe's fierceft fire,
Who dare live heedlefs of their country's ire;
With face ftrong-guarded to the blufh of fhame,
What virtue hates to hear they joy to name;
Mad with the rage of pleafure they refort,
The mimics, play'rs, and libertines of court;
In joys inglorious ev'ry fweet they rove,
And give their giddy fouls to mirth and love.
What tho' devoted to a fov'reign's rule
They trod the flow'ry paths of folly's fchool;

Spurn'd

Spurn'd what he hated, lov'd what he admir'd,
Thought as he thought, and fpoke as he infpir'd;
Far other cares a ftatefman's foul fhould guide,
Not the mean foothing of a monarch's pride.

Now grandeur frolics with more gen'rous rage,
And fpreads rich luftre on a graceful age;
Let Spain, enraptur'd at the well-known feaft,
With daring arm confront the madden'd beaft;
Th' attractive Bruifer fires with nobler charms,
Expert in ill he whirls his brawny arms;
His friend perhaps confronts the fatal blow,
His friend, for others' madnefs doom'd a foe.
Still glows the fcene, till mangled in the ftrife,
One hero gives the day, and oft his life.
Veil, veil the favage fhow, ye titled race,
Nor more the Briton and the Man difgrace;
Left mimics of the fword's politer fkill,
Thefe vagrants deem it honor's tafk to kill.

Tell me, ye gen'rous, whofe unfpotted foul
Dares what it thinks to fpeak without control,
Say, does not Cranmer richeft glories claim
(Cranmer, the martyr to religion's fame)
While Mary, Sin's detefted queen, is fcorn'd,
Tho' deck'd with fceptres, and with crowns adorn'd?
Oh, that the rage of injur'd Heav'n had fhed
Each fierceft torment on that impious head!

Low

Low from th' offended feat of empire thrown,
To pine in darknefs, and in dungeons groan!
A wretch whofe foul no fcenes of horror fhake,
The rack thy laughter, and thy jeft the ftake.

Far diff'rent thoughts the virgin-queen employ,
Not thus the flave of ev'ry brutal joy;
Firm devotee to virtue, and to right,
No terrors daunt her, and no threats affright.
Not hers the hands which ftain religion's flood
With favage flaughter, and a wafte of blood;
Not hers the heart to gen'rous deeds unknown,
Which leaps in rapture at the good man's groan.

Come then, thou tyrant of diftinguifh'd birth,
Strike up each note of harmony and mirth;
Roufe in a peal of joy each blithfome found,
Bedeck'd with fplendors, and with chaplets crown'd;
Come fatiate, if thou canft, thy glorying eyes,
And fwell with tranfport while the martyr dies.

What crimes inhuman Caledonia blot,
Tho' fons of grandeur crown the mighty plot!
See how they fwell, all-frantic in their ire,
To pour rebellion, and the ftate to fire!
See the fell bigots of enthufiaft zeal,
They rufh infatiate 'gainft the public weal,

To

To deeds which none but favage breafts would own,
No tears can expiate, and no pangs atone.
At length his fword refenting William draws,
Th' undaunted champion of his England's caufe;
Still facing danger with a manly fmile,
Till the full conqueft crowns his gen'rous toil.
Such, fuch the deeds which glory's foul enflame,
And fpread on Cefar's cheek the blufh of fhame;
Deeds which a kingdom's joys from tyrants fave,
Not gall the fubject, and the ftate enflave.

All-hail! to thee each gen'rous bofom falls,
Thee, William, favior of thy country calls;
To thee would honor richeft incenfe fhed,
Tho' from the cottage born, or defart bred.

'Twas thus that Edward, with a fond delight,
Rufh'd to the field, and trod the paths of fight:
Not his from toil his dauntlefs breaft to clofe,
Bold 'mid the thunder of furrounding foes;
Foremoft the foldiers' courage he infpir'd,
And knew no danger where his country fir'd.

Immortal Creffy, Edward's worth proclaim,
Sound forth his glories, and enlarge his fame;
Thou too, Poictiers, the champion's deeds difplay,
And fwell the terrors of thy fatal day;

4

When,

When, the triumphant victor of the war,
Imperial captives grac'd his mighty car.

Nor thefe alone fair grandeur's glories fpread,
Lo ! other heroes rear their laurel'd head ;
I fee in radiance to my dazzled eyes
The mighty fhades of conqu'ring Henries rife ;
Who virtue's vot'ries crown'd with triumph glow
Their country's pride, and terror of the foe.
With princely worth the Royal Youth * had fhewn,
'Tho' thoufand Wills had driv'n him from the throne ;
Had fate but fpar'd thee in the bloom of youth,
That arm, the pillar of religious truth,
Had bid the realm on virtue's pinions foar,
And clos'd with rig'rous force oppreffion's door ;
Alike religion's and his country's fhield,
Pride of the council, glory of the field.
No Bonner, monfter of the Popifh caufe,
With haughty ftride had trampled o'er the laws ;
No pope prefumptuous at a queen's command
Had hurl'd deftruction o'er the bleeding land ;
Quafh'd by the frenzy of the fons of pride,
Nor truth had fuffer'd, nor had Cranmer dy'd.

Who pants for battle at his country's call,
Who quells the Spaniard, and controls the Gaul,

* Edward VI.

Whofe

Whofe gen'rous life confpicuous glories grace,
His honor's poft—I care not for his race ;
Him chief of fav'rites grandeur's voice will own,
And fpurn a Cromwell feated on a throne.
On him be fhow'r'd the titles of the great,
Not thee who loll'ft in lux'ry's lifelefs ftate ;
A wretch, who loft to ev'ry fpark of fame,
Spring'ft from oblivion, and ufurp'ft a name ;
Perhaps fome Wolfey (damn'd to bafe renown)
Fly'ft from the flaughter-houfe to feize a crown.

THE

THE

NINTH SATIRE

IMITATED.

FRIEND.

WHY droops thy foul with confcious grief op-
  prefs'd.?
Why ftarts the tear, and heaves the penfive
  breaft?
Demure thou ftalk'ft in melancholy fate,
Like fome difcarded minifter of ftate;
Not Heath——e's felf, whofe folemn footfteps range,
Proud to be fam'd the wealthieft of the Change,
So mourn'd, when not a dupe enrich'd the day,
And not one fpendthrift-ftripling was his prey.

Thy

Thy fneers of old wit's fallies could excite
'Gainſt the rude toſſing of a new-made knight;
Could dwell admiring on the charms which yields
To RURAL cits the proſpect of Moorfields.
Now plung'd in thought, and fix'd in deep deſpair,
Fix'd as in gloomy mathematic care;
No more, alas! can friendſhip's fondneſs ſpy
Health in thy cheek, and laughter in thine eye;
No more the well-trim'd treſſes' poliſh'd grace,
But a dead ſorrow, furrows o'er thy face.
Yet vain the falt'ring footſteps' borrow'd art,
The glowing fever's agonizing ſmart;
Friendſhip, alas! the true diſeaſe can find,
The lurking pangs of a deſpondent mind.

Can ſtreams roll backward from their ancient ſource,
Or o'er the mountain bend their wayward courſe?
No—and ſhall man in varying circles range,
The ſon of reaſon, yet the ſlave of change?
Ere-while you ſhone at mirth's enchanting call,
The grace, the glory of the glitt'ring ball;
Tho' deck'd with Strode the dance, the piercing dart
Glanc'd from your eyes to ev'ry virgin's heart.

F L O R I O.

When youth's high blood ran rev'ling in my vein,
I glow'd the chief ('tis true) of pleaſure's train;

The

The jovial vot'ry of each gay delight,
The day I frolic'd, and I lov'd the night :
But glutted now, the dear-bought joys I mourn
Of wretches lately whom I fed the fcorn ;
Wretches, with grace tho' others' aid they ufe,
Their own, which once they proffer'd, who refufe.
In vain to well-known boards my fteps I bend,
Doom'd to no treat, and welcome to no friend ;
My purfe rich-founding in my hour of fin
Scarce feels a folitary piece within ;
The lov'd affociates of my happier day,
Loathing a beggar'd brother, flink away.
Of old, they cry, the merrieft fons of earth,
We ranfack'd ev'ry clime for joy and mirth ;
Flufh'd with the rapt'rous fweets of riot fhone,
Nor envy'd monarchs glitt'ring on the throne ;
But now how droop'ft thou, Florio ? doom'd no more
To drain the bowl, and ply the midnight roar ;
Still fix'd in woe thy moments to employ ;—
No fon of poverty's the fon of joy.

Are thefe the fouls, who link'd in friendfhip's chain,
Brothers in blifs, and partners of my reign,
Shar'd EV'N my ALL, when profp'rous moments blefs'd ;
To whom I op'd each fecret of my breaft ?
What fiends to fpurn with looks of angry hate,
Who firft reduc'd me to this haplefs ftate !

K   Eternal

Eternal truth they vow'd—I blefs'd the hour,
And cherifh'd friends, who meant but to devour.
Thofe yellow treafures of the mountain's brow
(Once Florio's wealth, alas! another's now)
The fragrant meads, the gurgling river's fall,
To thefe how often welcom'd, and to all!
For them alone I liv'd—for them my board
Lavifh I fpread—for them unlock'd my hoard;
Yes, they were welcome, tho' my wealth's amount
The fiends of change had labor'd to recount;
For them the voice ungrateful I defpis'd,
Which fafety's fane thro' virtue's path advis'd.

F R I E N D.

Say, why exhauft the wealth which crown'd thy birth
On carelefs faunt'rers, on the drones of earth?
As fondly fir'd to piety and knowledge,
Sir Jacob left his all to build a college.
Prefumptuous fouls to afk—'tis true you plead
That youth and friendfhip led you to the deed.

F L O R I O.

Yes, friendfhip blinded, and unthinking youth
O'erpow'r'd the voice of reafon and of truth.
This friend's diftrefs'd, I muft fupply his want;
Another deep in debt—relief I grant.

Not

Not like the cautious ant I kept my ſtore,
Ere ſadden'd winter's frown beſieg'd my door;
But now it low'rs; my purſe exhauſted fails,
Almoſt the ſilver for my Chriſtmas vails:
What can be done? afflicted Florio give
Th' advice he oft has ſlighted to receive.

FRIEND.

Juſt is thy grief; and will the monſters ſhew
No kind regard, no pity to thy woe?

FLORIO.

Away, they cry, thou deſtitute of pelf,
Others there are as thoughtleſs as thyſelf;
Yes, there are thoſe (ye poor men turn aſide)
Thoughtleſs as Florio, and with wealth beſide.
Theſe frolic ſlutt'rers, inſolently gay,
Who ſpin thro' life, and fritter time away,
To worth diſtreſs'd can ſharpeſt pangs impart,
And thoſe who ſhar'd the boſom ſting the heart.
So lumpiſh S—l—n, with ſcarce common ſenſe,
The headpiece ſtupifies to ſteal the pence;
(Standing like dullneſs' ſelf demurely prim)
As ſurgeons numb you ere they lop the limb.

FRIEND.

FRIEND.

Alas! my injur'd friend, no kind difguife
Can fcreen thy riches from the harpy's eyes;
Flutt'ring in gaiety, elate with health,
The fteeds, the car proclaim the man of wealth;
The menial train, the column-ftructur'd dome
Befpeak no prefent poverty at home.
Yet fhut the windows, clofe the rigid door,
Seem to the world the pooreft of the poor;
Stop ev'ry chink, nor eye, nor lift'ning ear,
Pore on thy fecrets, or thy whifpers hear;
Vain is the care; what circling tongues conceal,
Ev'n walls themfelves will fpeak, and bolts reveal:
To prying man the confcious truth impart,
And flatt'ring crowds will bellow what thou art.

Fir'd by th' alluring train, at once you need
A letter'd treafure, tho' you fcarce can read;
French cooks befiege the gate with cringing view,
Which but before the fimpleft diet knew.
A coxcomb now complete you ftrut about,
And join the polifh'd world's fantaftic rout;
Scoff'd by the peer, whofe lifping modes you prize,
While ev'n the wretches whom you feed defpife.

When

When to the great, my Florio, you refort,
The friend invites you only for his fport;
Drink is the word; you quaff with thoughtlefs breaft,
Till the gorg'd drunkard crowns the wanton jeft.
Thus Florio falls; to ev'ry friend they meet
They roar your folly, and proclaim the feat;
With warmer ftrains their tranfports they reveal
Than prieftly knaves, whofe hypocritic zeal
Seeks the fond rabble's ign'rant fouls to move,
Then fly with rapture to their feafts of love.

Dare be thyfelf—at once thy conduct fave
From the pert noble, and the perter flave;
Thus may you fpurn the prattling, fcoffing fool,
Curs'd with a tongue, without a head to rule.
What fouls from fuch would feel th' infulting fneer,
From whom they've nought to hope, and nought to fear!
Favor'd by Heav'n, I can enjoy my board,
Nor heed the pamper'd flave, or giddy lord;
Can fee dependant peers with pitying view,
And keep that counfel I impart to you.

F L O R I O,

Alas! 'twere well; were mine that gen'rous boaft,
Could I retrieve thofe moments I have loft,
Florio were blefs'd!—I'll feize the circling time,
And crufh in age the follies of my prime.

K 3

Thou

Thou time, like fortune, conftant but in change,
Thou flutt'ring pow'r, delighting ftill to range,
In giddy courfe whofe carelefs pinions fpring,
A moving zephyr, ever on the wing;
Giv'ft momentary peace, and fleeting ftrife,
Nor heed'ft the farce and lottery of life.
Mark! while the bowl difplays its jovial round,
The glowing front while rofy wreaths furround,
While flufh'd with love, time haftens to deftroy
The feaft of rapture, and o'erwhelm our joy.

Grant me, kind Heav'n! to whofe indulgent pow'r
I oft have fhed the pray'r's devoted fhow'r,
Grant me to live my little being's fpan,
To blefs the world, and know myfelf a man;
Far, far remove difeafe's painful rage,
That fureft enfign of protracted age.
Let others brooding o'er their chefts behold
Unnumber'd filver, and exhauftlefs gold;
Whofe high-pil'd ftore, tho' ravifh'd with the prize,
Would pall the grim excifeman's greedy eyes.
I afk no gilded car's unwieldy weight,
Which forms an aukward mayor's uncomely ftate;
Whofe fhallow parts but fix the price of bread,
And ill-penn'd periods to the fov'reign fhed.

Yet—one, one humble lux'ry I defire,
That the warm'd mufe may catch congenial fire;

I afk

I afk fome learned buft, whofe rev'rend looks
May fmile a fanction to my circling books ;
Then, but how fond the wifh ! thy pow'rful frown,
Whofe blaft can fink a monarch to a clown,
Thy frown may well the lov'd requeft deny,
For now my humbleft wifh afpires too high :
Afpires ! (yet Heav'n indulge the bounded flame)—
Deaf to ambition's fong, be mine an honeft fame.

THE

THE

TENTH SATIRE

IMITATED.

FAR from the rifing to the fetting day
 Let reafon dart her intellectual ray;
 How few, tho' panting with a keen delight,
 Tread with triumphant zeal the paths of right!
Full o'er the heart the clouds of error rife,
And paffion's phantoms fwim before our eyes;
Vain hopes, or vainer terrors feize the foul,
Tho' wifdom's lamp would light us to the goal.
Turn to ambition, lo! deftruction fpreads
From darling counfels on the ftatefmens' heads;
Self-murd'ring erudition damns the gown,
And death hangs low'ring o'er a chief's renown.

Ye

Ye fons of eloquence, attentive fit,
Fir'd by the torrent of undaunted Pitt ;
Then view that torrent crufh'd by Scotifh hate,
View it, and truckle to a flave of ftate.
Severer horrors blaft the mifer's reft ;
The famifh'd harpy hov'ring o'er the cheft
For gilded mountains barters fame and health,
And proudly boafts the world a flave to wealth.

At this dread feafon, when at B—e's command
Thick crowds of Northerns blacken all the land ;
When nobles, exil'd to their rural feat,
Shine in the milder fplendors of retreat ;
What ruling paffion fires the gaping race ?—
Nought wooes the patriot, but the vacant place.
Elfe ftill in fordid poverty at home
Still the proud courtier o'er his wilds might roam ;
Still might the bonnet, as of late unknown
Difgrace Plebeïans, not befiege the th——e.
But now, triumphant o'er Culloden's day,
It darts its horrors to the folar ray ;
Crouch'd to the mighty Baal England fee,
And to the want she gilded, bend her knee.

Impatient all for wealth, for honors cry,
For thefe we pour the pray'r, we heave the figh ;
Each the low flave of grandeur, and of pelf,
Damns ev'ry neighbor greater than himfelf.

Yet

Yet poifon blafts not in the lowly cot,
Such horrors only are ambition's lot ;
Unknown to me, it fhakes th' exalted foul,
Glows in his feaft, and mingles with his bowl.

Fir'd at the fchemes of ftate, one Englifh fage
Laughs at the northern dotage of the age;
Quick taunts of humor aid the gen'ral cry,
While others only anfwer with a figh ;
The laughter's eafy ; but what forrow fills
The mighty meafure of a kingdom's ills !

Arife, oh ! genius, and my bofom lift
To the full fpirit of a freeborn Swift ;
The friend of nature, and the foul of whim,
Fools, knaves, or ftatefmen, all the fame to him.
Oh ! had he feen, to feed his ftreaming hate,
A northern Galba foaring on the ft—e !
Seen the triumphant Jehu fcour the land,
Grac'd with rich trappings from preferment's hand ;
Seen the bright ftar's, the pompous title's ray,
Each gewgaw op'ning to the face of day !
Still fwell'd, and pamper'd with redoubled ftore,
Till peace, peace only could procure him more :—
In that the high-tax'd B—f—d gives him eafe ;
B—f—d our alien ftatefman born to pleafe.

But lo ! his grace's coftly train advance,
Wafted triumphant to the realms of France ;
Encircling minions form his fplendid boaft,
And fhatter'd Gallia hails him to her coaft ;
Proceed, ye tribes, fuch fcenes a R——y fuit,
Whom place and penfion make a flave to B———.

Yes, daring Swift, infpire the glowing ftrain ;
Let crowded follies feed th' eternal vein ;
Th' indignant ftreams o'er upftart grandeur roll,
Where art's, not wifdom's, dictates fill the foul ;
Yes ! ftill unaw'd the mighty vulgar fcare,
Nor wooe the fruits of Caledonian air.
As flam'd of old thy fatire's boundlefs fong
To point a C—t—t to th' indignant throng.

The fmiles of folly, and the ftings of pride,
The giddy foul to fatal wifhes guide ;
See panting grandeur all her fnares impart,
(Th' eternal banquet to an envious heart)
This hour the nation's love, the next her hate,
Sunk are her titles, wither'd all her ftate ;
Lamenting only for themfelves her doom,
Walk forth the ftatues of the levee-room ;
Statues, till now for ever rooted there,
Seek the kind influence of a warmer air :
Th' inceffant curfe the victim's fteps attends,
And the ftorm thunders on his guiltlefs friends.

3

Now

Now—the lov'd idol of the kingdom fee,
Scourg'd by vile hands, or burnt in effigy;
Torn from each houfe behold the fav'rite face
To the next upftart fool refigns its place;
That face accuftom'd next its prince to fhine,
Daub'd for a cot, or plaifter'd for a fign.

Ye fons of pow'r (fuch themes your genius fit)
Blaft the retirement of the patriot P— :
Say, that his foul with thirft of flaughter glows;
That gold and peerage lead him by the nofe;
Unfit for bus'nefs from eternal gout,
Say, you ne'er lov'd him, and rejoice he's OUT.

Whence, ruthlefs cenfor, ftreams the rude difgrace?
What crime? what guilt? proclaim it to his face.
'Twas this: He nobly fcorn'd that Britain's reign
Should fall a victim to the frauds of Spain.
Afk of the ftatefmen, who purfu'd his plan,
Afk of the people, for they know the man;
Thefe cannot liften to the c—tly call,
They know; they love him better from his fall:
And ftill, for George to footh the nation's groan,
Their vows had kept this ftatefman near the throne,
Infpir'd by thefe behold th' attractive fhow'r
Rolls to the Favorite from the SOUL of pow'r,
The foul thrice happy in domeftic peace;—
Oh, may the genial tranfports never ceafe!

But

But ah ! what demon fans the rifing fire !
The beft, the greateft of the realm retire ;
Difgufted patriots fwell the public jar,
Chiefs of the council, heroes of the war.
Stand faft, O Galba ! and fuftain the blow,
Wrap'd in thy circling votaries fpurn the foe ;
Rivet ambition on the bafe of gain,
Proof to the tumults of the murm'ring train ;
And deem the clamors, which thy pow'r difown,
Sprung from the frenzy of the mob alone.
But fay, reflection, would thy awful nod
Swell with the glories of this earthly god ;
Thy kinfmen fill each office of the ftate,
While fword, law, gofpel, at thy levee wait ?
From thee fhall England's treafures iffue forth,
To glut the defarts of the darling North ?
Yes—thou would'ft feed with tales a fondling k—g ;
Yes—thou would'ft hold the nation in a ftring ;
Ambition, av'rice, pride, thy bofom fill,
Charms which o'erpow'r the fafcinated will :—
Yet, yet the fummit of thy wifhes gain ;
The joy's ideal only, fix'd the pain.

Ah ! rather vaunting from inferior parts,
Ply in the city's gloom mechanic arts :
Thy drudging foul for fneaking knav'ry known,
Let pamper'd dullnefs mark thee for her own.

Ye flaves of ftate, whofe fteps inebriate roam,
Flufh'd with the fplendors of ambition's dome;
Too foon ye mourn deftruction's fatal found,
And the huge ftructure thund'ring to the ground;
Sink from the tow'ring height, and crufh'd below,
Curfe your wild frenzy in the depths of woe.

Whence wither'd droops a W—lp—le's fully'd fame?
Who rous'd or check'd at will the patriot's flame;
With parts from nature's genuine bounty great,
Thro' frauds he courted, and maintain'd his ftate;
Till ferreted from pow'r, in quiet laid,
He purchas'd fafety in the title's fhade.
How rarely vet'rans from the ftorms of ftrife
Unfully'd walk into the vale of life!

Flufh'd by a P—lt—ey's ftrain the parent calls
The fprightly youth to academic walls;
The folemn tutor, with an aukward grace,
Steel'd to the native dullnefs of the place,
In Euclid's labyrinth damps th'afpiring rage,
Flounder'd in fcience's mechanic page.
Yet wifer HE—ambition choak'd the flame,
And title clips the wings of P—lt—ey's fame.
Holles' fuperior fplendors feaft his eyes,
Whofe broken notes lift Granta to the fkies:
" Tho' well at court your loyalty is known,
" I vow I muft commend it to the throne."

Yet

Yet vainly, Granta, flow thefe artlefs ftrains,
When thirfty B—e flies panting to the reins;
Vainly or wit or dullnefs fhield his grace,
B—e cares not for his fpeeches, but his place.

Ev'n HE fits driv'ling o'er life's ling'ring end,
He whom aufpicious virtue ftamp'd her friend;
Whofe dauntlefs torrent on corruption roll'd,
And pour'd the venom o'er the flaves of gold;
Warm from the city's fmiles, this truly great
This honor'd father * flew to fhield the ftate;
Sufpends each humbler care from traffic fprung,
And freedom's dictates animate his tongue.

Ye fons of war, triumphant from your toils,
Flufh'd with rich trophies, and adorn'd with fpoils,
For whom fack'd kingdoms pour the captive train,
Lords of the field, and fov'reigns of the main,
How glows the conqueft flaming to your eyes!
Swells in the foul, and lifts you to the fkies.
For this undaunted at the fcene of wars
Ye laugh at fear, and glory in your fcars;
O'er Greece, o'er Rome your country's fplendors raife,
So boils this ardor of immortal praife!
Immortal praife, which fafcinates the mind,
While virtue unregarded lags behind.

* Sir John Barnard.

Ev'n

Ev'n some, pufh'd onward by fermenting blood,
Have crufh'd each barrier of their country's good;
Ambition's fiends, like ruthlefs Cromwell, own
No folid joy that fmiles beneath a throne.
But think'ft thou, Tyrant, that the vaunting buft,
The lying marble, confecrates thy duft?
Lac'd with infcription, and fring'd round with fhew,
While hift'ry damns the wretch who fleeps below.

See Pruffian might o'er hofts combin'd prevail,
And poife each fplendid deed in reafon's fcale;
That king, the terror of Germania's plains,
No conqueft fatiates, and no foe contains;
In vain protected by the maze of art,
Saxonia feels the arrow in her heart;
In vain encumber'd with her thoufand hands,
Ruffia huge elephant of battle ftands;
Nor art nor nature checks his headlong fway,
Nor batt'ries damp his fire, nor ramparts ftay;
O'er flaming Prague the thund'ring engines roll,
Bohemia fhudders thro' her inmoft foul.
" Yet ftill (he cries) th'infatiate blaze fhall fhine,
" Till the full conqueft call Silefia mine;
" Till falfe Vienna Pruffia's wrongs requite,
" And ftreams of flaughter waft me to my right."

Still this avenging thunderbolt of war
Deftruction fcatters from ambition's car;
L

Fam'd

Fam'd as in conqueft, manly in retreat,
Bold from his errors, dreadful in defeat;
No flight inglorious ftamps degen'rate fears,
No bafe conceffion, and no daftard tears.
Tho' boundlefs av'rice kindles Sweden's arms,
And Auftria thunders to the dire alarms;
On Poland's realm imperial lightnings fall,
And ruin low'rs on Berlin's fav'rite wall:
With rage recruited Fred'ric's arms advance,
Thy day, great Rofbach, lives the curfe of France;
The fierce enthufiafm * fan'd by fov'reign breath
Eggs on the warriors, and enflames to death.

With thirft infatiate rolls ambition's mind,
Enrag'd to conqueft, and in camps confin'd;
Still coop'd and fetter'd in imprifon'd ftate,
The world itfelf's too bounded for his hate.
Again to battle headftrong Auftria calls;
Daun with a figh retires, and Breflau falls.
But fay, what period checks the warrior's cares?
Their fatal goal's the death he greatly dares:
There lodg'd, no more ambition's fpirits roam,
A fhroud her treafure, and the earth her home.

Nor deem romantic fancy cheats your eyes,
When toils on toils the mighty foul defies;

---

* King of Pruffia's fpirited fpeech before the battle of Rofbach.

Squadrons

Squadrons whofe thirft collected ftreams can drain,
Whofe hunger defolate th' extended plain;
Squadrons who more demand the poet's care,
Than bloated Henry's wire-drawn by Voltaire.

See Swedifh madnefs pour o'er Ruffia's coaft,
Bound in the chains of adamantine froft;
He combats fea and air at glory's founds,
Spurns the wide ramparts, and o'erleaps the mounds;
Himfelf a mighty hoft, he gives the nod,
United millions tremble to the rod.
But mark, misfortunes crufh the wild defire;
See the fell comet fetting worlds on fire,
Who proudly deems an hero's foul defign'd
The fcourge, and not the blefling of mankind;
See him, whofe fury had deform'd the fhore
With hills of corfes, and with feas of gore,
Fall'n in inglorious ftrife ambition's prey,
To a mean random arm refign the day.

O ye! ftill panting for increafe of care,
Who pour for length of days th' eternal pray'r,
Paufe o'er the wretched hofpital of age,
Where mis'ries heap'd on mis'ries feaft their rage;
Where finks the manly feature's healthful glow,
Nor fcarce humanity's remains can fhew;
Abforb'd in furrows, blafted ev'ry grace,
More coarfe, more baleful than a Northern face,

L 2

When the rude cub the fondling parent greets,
And warm ideas promife England's fweets.
In varying youth we different charms admire,
Th' attractive form, or more attractive fire;
Age droops for ever hateful, ftill the fame,
The fhiv'ring voice, lank jaw, and palfy'd frame;
Not of a body, but a corfe poffefs'd;
The nofe—let decency conceal the reft.
A meer excrefcence he ufurps the light,
Him wife and children view with aching fight;
A curfe to all, a torment to himfelf,—
Stand to your tafk, ye fycophants of pelf.

In vain the goblet's purple treafures roll,
Each fweet of lux'ry palls upon the foul;
In vain the ftage extends her magic charms,
No mirth allures him, and no woe difarms;
Trumpet nor drum his deaden'd fenfe can hear,
But thro' the friendly trumpet at his ear:
Yet—leave thefe paftimes to the living train,
Nor fhew with want of ears thy want of brain.
Languidly creeping life's dull channels know
No wak'ning ardor, but the fever's glow;
The reft an ague all, whofe tremor fills,
And ftamps the mighty magazine of ills;
Ills o'er the dregs of life whofe horrors fit,
In crowds unnumber'd as the friends of PITT,

As priefts expectant who befieg'd his grace,
Now flown by nature to the next in place ;
Or ftructures rear'd by pride (a coftly train)
Rear'd on the ruins of Culloden's plain.

The crippled martyr view ; his cens'ring tongue,
The fole remaining member, damns the young ;
Befet with pains himfelf, he hates the free,—
Stone-blind himfelf, he rails at thofe who fee.
Dines he abroad ? befide his feeder ftands,
Helplefs he lives but by another's hands.
Of old his fenfes lux'ry's board could greet,
Now flacken'd nature flumbers o'er the treat ;
Officious parafites with friendly plan
Fly to regale,—and choak him if they can.

Severer doom the wretched clod attends,
Ignorance alike of fervants, and of friends ;
Ign'rant or carelefs of the child he bred,
His will leaves all to Lucy in his ftead ;
Infidious harlot ! whofe triumphant art
To doting age love's opiates can impart.

But grant that reafon's lamp, whofe genial ray
Illum'd the conduct of his earlier day,
Grant that this lamp with undiminifh'd fires
The peaceful virtues of his age infpires ;

Yet

Yet circling mis'ries claim the kindred tear,
Wife, brother, fister, lead the crowded bier;
Familiar death the ling'ring vet'ran scares,
Far lefs by age diftinguifh'd than by cares.

For proofs on Homer's fong my mufe could call
(Nor deem, ye Northerns, that I mean Fingal)
Could raife up many a hero, who out-ran
By many a year th' accuftom'd date of man;
Heroes, who chatting o'er unnumber'd bowls,
Drank their fair laffes, and enlarg'd their fouls.
Could thence attend them to life's clofing fcene,
And point the joylefs victims of chagrin;
Shew fons, wives, daughters, mounted on the pyre,
—Then envy, if you can, the widow'd fire;
The fire who loathing his protracted breath,
From Heav'n's indulgence waits the ftroke of death.
Let Grecian vet'rans view, immers'd in pain,
Their offspring hurry'd to the Trojan plain;
Drop we the theme, by ev'ry fchool-boy known,
And view (for once) examples of our own.

Had Scottifh James beheld the clofe of life,
Crufh'd in fome petty Caledonian ftrife;
Toil'd to his end a pirate o'er the main,
Nor curs'd with Stuart hatred England's reign;
Blefs'd were my country;—on his native fhore
Some bluft'ring bard his elegy might roar;

Some

Some Romiſh prieſt have clos'd him in his bier,
And his own REAL children dropt a tear.

But ſprung from him the Scots' collected ire
Spreads the loath'd kingdom with rebellion's fire;
T' aſſert an upſtart's viſionary right
The plaided murd'rers ruſh their friends to fight:
Unſheath'd the falchion beams in William's arm;
Culloden lives to ſpeak the dread alarm.
Culloden, may no years thy mem'ry blot!
Live, ever live to curſe the haughty Scot.
For thee, O William! whoſe unſully'd praiſe
Each patriot-ſoul ſhall ever dare to raiſe,
Thy worth the conſecrating muſe ſhall ſpeak,
Tho' ribbald Scotſmen ſplit their envious cheek;
Still will thy conqueſts hail, unaw'd by f——e,
Nor fear the venom of a Northern hate.

'Twas thus the ſenior's winter low'r'd of old;
Stamp'd in each rolling age the proofs behold;
In each the crowds of ancient wretches ſhew,
Man vainly dreams of happineſs below.
Diſgraceful woes in Somers' exile view,
See adverſe fate the man of worth purſue:
In tears, religion, mourn thy loſt ſupport;
In tears, O juſtice, mourn thy beggar'd court.
Somers in virtue, as in wiſdom great,
Shone on th' exalted pinnacle of ſtate;

There

There pity ſtreaming from his godlike breaſt
From venal vengeance ſuccor'd the diſtreſs'd;
That venal vengeance, whoſe wild torrent ſprings,
And tears the ſtateſman from the beſt of kings.
Bleſs'd in retirement by the public pray'r,
He quits in Cheſhunt's ſhade the load of care;
Yet there diſeaſe's agonizing prey,
Fell dotage blaſts the ev'ning of his day.
Happy in this; amid corruption's train
He bad fair virtue beam on England's reign;
Lov'd of the people, darling of the throne,
Nor great, like others, for himſelf alone:
Praiſe, ye dire St. Johns, praiſe th' illuſtrious bier,
And learn the ſons of virtue to revere.

For beauty on her ſons the mother cries,
But for her dearer daughter rends the ſkies;
By rapid zeal to frenzy's ſtrains betray'd,
Ev'n now ſhe feels the damſel's fortune made.
But ah! what miſchiefs frown on beauty's ſcene!
Turn, calm reflection, turn to H——r's mien;
Who ſadly curs'd with each attractive grace,
Had liv'd more happy with a grandame's face.

But chief when beauty decks the lovely boy,
Cares heap'd on cares the parent's peace annoy;
Crowds of temptations choak the narrow road
That leads to modeſty's ſerene abode.

Tho'

Tho' education's rigid lore diſplays
The full-blown dignity of ancient days,
Tho' nature ſtreaks him with her genuine flame,
And the bluſh kindles to the hint of blame,
(Nature, whoſe dictates purer wiſdom wear
Than the dull moraliſt's affected care)
See thro' the world officious friends combin'd,
And luring pleaſures ſteal away the mind ;
Vice fires the paſſions with a fond regard,
Till baffled virtue ſighing quits her guard.

For you, ye fair, whoſe unreſiſted charms
Win the full crowd of victims to your arms,
Lo ! fatal poiſon buſy love imparts,
Your very ſwains the traitors of your hearts ;
Each look, each thought repeated rivals blame,
And plant their vengeful batt'ries at your fame.

Nor ill the torrent to the maid apply'd,
Whoſe ſilly heart is vaſſal to her pride ;
Who deeming all a conqueſt to her eyes,
Gives to the wealthy fool the ſacred prize ;
While worth in vain ſits ſighing for her charms,
And beauty's bury'd in an upſtart's arms.

Mark now the ſuitor's ſlav'ry to the fair ;
In form the maiden, ſmirking in her chair,

Receives

Receives the youth ; ten thoufand vifits paid,
Her worth (or fortune) is at laft difplay'd ;
For Smithfield-parents, tho' they fcarce can fcore,
In THIS well know that two and two make four.
And now poor Cloe muft her mind reveal,
For fee around the lawyer, prieft, and feal ;
Here too the ufeful priefts their aid impart,
Tho' in all elfe fhe hates them to the heart.
If once ere this a fav'ring flame fhe own,
Swift flies officious fcandal through the town ;
(Scandal which aggravates thy foft defire,
When correfpondence fans the giddy fire)
Her lover's vanity the buz attends,
And fwears her fondnefs to his goffip-friends ;
The friends with fhouts the coxcomb's lie improve,
And all, all cry, poor Cloe is in love.
Fan'd by their baleful breath the cenfures roll,
And a fool's treach'ry ftabs you to the foul.

Say then, muft man no fondling wifhes fhed,
Left troops of evils thunder on his head ?
Fix'd in a ftagnant lethargy of fcene,
No active paffion rouze the dull machine ?
Away—let calm content infpire thy breaft,
And Heav'n, thy dearer friend, difpofe the reft ;
Heav'n, whofe mild influ'nce checks our frantic fires,
And reins the headlong torrent of defires ;

5

That

That eye, to each unfashion'd secret known,
That eye, which ever wakes for man alone.
Yet, still expectant of its guardian care,
Pour the sweet incense of obedient pray'r;
For health's warm glow let strong devotion roll,
To wake to life each virtue of the soul.
The soul serene, whose steady smiles attend,
Prop'd by religion, thine approaching end;
The soul no fears appal, no labors tire;
No dupe to rage, no captive to desire;
Which flush'd like Tillotson with virtue's blaze,
Spurns the dull flutter of a Charles's days.

    Thus beams the native dignity of man;
Rise—mount with ardor to the gen'rous plan;
Let sacred prudence light thee in thy way,
Prudence to virtue fan'd by wisdom's ray,
There fix resolv'd; there, proof to fortune's charms,
Go—spurn the fickle phantom from thy arms.

THE

ELEVENTH SATIRE

IMITATED.

IF. lordly Bute difplay the fplendid feafts,
Courtiers his vaffals, freeholders his guefts;
While fhouting Scots ftand gaping at his gate,
We think him lib'ral, for his name is great.
Th' expenfive treat if M——dl——n employ
To feed the palate of the royal boy,
'Tis folly, ALL exclaim, to fpend our ftore
To furnifh princes, when ourfelves are poor.

How finks mean Wharton in the rolls of fame
Let brothels tell, which oft have roar'd his name;
Tho' form'd by nature for the patriot's care,
In peace to govern, and direct in war,

This

This wanton Clodio of the courtly train,
While youth's high blood ran rev'ling in his vein,
Urg'd by caprice, by fancy's whims control'd,
Drop'd in a ftew the gen'rous and the bold;
And, on a harlot's fofter breaft reclin'd,
Drove honor, worth, and reafon from his mind;
Skill'd in the bow'rs of vice each hour t' improve,
And all his being s end to laugh and love.

Far better Gay, who firm in virtuous pride,
Tho' one poor meal fcarce able to provide,
Lafh'd follies glaring in the fons of birth,
His only bulwarks Queenfbury and worth.

But THESE o'er nature's fpace for lux'ry pore,
For ever thoughtlefs to difcharge the fcore;
Thefe their own country fpurn with polifh'd breaft,
To them the deareft only is the beft.
To quit th' expences of their fumptuous ftate,
Firft for their debts' difcharge they melt their plate;
The next thofe objects of their fonder view
(Not of their tafte) the fplendors of virtu
Sink for a nought; then iffuing on the ftage,
They mimic lavifh lux'ry's well-known rage.

Not fo the peer; let debts furround him ftill,
No fortune HIS to fhudder at a bill;

Tho'

Tho' loads of duft th' expectant Papers draw,
Heap'd as the parchment-fcriblings of the law;
Yet ftill he builds, ftill faunters void of cares,
Fix'd in himfelf, for no arreft he fears.

Man, know thyfelf; with all perfuafion's art
How fink the founds their paffage to my heart!
Would this direct us to the beauteous wife,
And fway th' inferior offices of life;
Would this direct us to the field of war,
And rear us to the fenate or the bar;
To grace our ifle would other Marlb'roughs rife,
And PITTS fucceffive bloom before our eyes.

Come, my bold orator, with dauntlefs will
Confront a minifter's illegal bill;
Yet heed, left rambling in a wayward dream
Thy heated foul ftart wanton from the theme;
Let thoughtful judgment rein thy patriot-zeal,
Let judgment regulate domeftic weal.
What fools! who range the world for healthlefs food,
When cheaper England could procure as good;
Fools! foon to mourn their wealth-confuming tafte,
Of want the victims, and by worth difgrac'd.
See the laft fhilling comes demurely flow,
A long dead void th' exhaufted pockets fhew;
Like his, from vanity whofe loffes fpring,
And rob the preacher of his diamond-ring.

Well

Well may we dread (thus funk his abject ftate)
What moft he calls for—his untimely fate.

Such fafhion's fcenes; from folly's haplefs nights
The gold rolls plenteous at the den of Whites;
There lie the ftores in fplendid heaps difplay'd,
Tho' the poor taylor's bill remains unpaid.

But lo! at laft the lavifh treafure flown,
The gay Weft-Indian hurries from the town;
O'er diftant feas thofe fons of pleafure roam,
Their prefence needful for affairs at home;
The frolic champions with as carelefs foul
The dang'rous ocean plough from pole to pole,
As flaunting ladies fly from ftreet to ftreet,
Or city traders to a new-bought feat.
This, this the heart-felt pang, the galling care,
To quit for fwarthy loves the tender fair;
To leave (what thought can bear) the park, the play,
For the loath'd heat of a Jamaica-day.

Yet hence, enthufiafts, from our darling coaft
No worth with fuch, no modefty is loft;
Sworn foes to reafon, indolence's tools,
Whom frantic pride directs, and paffion rules.

But thou, my friend, each taunt of anger wreak
If what my heart conceives I dare not fpeak;

Slave

Slave of deceit proclaim me, if thou fee
One faithlefs deed with virtue difagree.
Come to my board, the friendly feaft is fpread,
No formal grin, no modifh cringes dread;
No—I will hail thee with a welcome look,
And treat thee far more gladly than a duke;
Too poor to fmile upon my friend, and pray,
That Heav'n had guided him a diff'rent way.

See! my whole treat is from my fields fupply'd,
I feek no market to indulge my pride;
A kid far fofter than the velvet-plain
Salutes my board, felected from the train;
Which doom'd the victim of this feftal day,
No more its parent fooths with fportive play.
Two tender chicks, oft fed from Florio's arm,
Clofe-pacing round the dame, fecure of harm,
Bleed for the treat; two others yonder fee,
Doom'd for a fecond treat, and doom'd to thee.
Cull'd from my humble garden's fruitful wall
The clufter's willing juices hail my call;
The downy peach in ruddy charms difplay'd,
Almoft a rival of the rofe-cheek'd maid,
Spreads its foft fweets; and, for a future feaft,
The healthier pippin ripens to thy tafte;
Still doom'd to triumph, tho' excis'd by B——,
Who loaths the fweets of ev'ry Englifh fruit.

M   Such

Such meals of old adorn'd the frugal board,
And pleas'd the palate of the greateſt lord ;
Of old the member, lov'd in his retreat,
Spent ev'ry Chriſtmas at his country-ſeat ;
Earth's choiceſt herbs the rural table grac'd,
Congenial to the tenants' honeſt taſte.
Such goodly modes no more engage the land,
They know no fare but from the ſervant's hand.
When the flitch'd bacon hung in pomp on high,
How did it joy the toiling farmer's eye !
The ſteward then, not inſolent as now,
The gueſt reſpected with a welcome bow ;
To all alike a willing ear he gave,
For then no maſter was his ſteward's ſlave :
They ſing, they count the triumphs of the plain,
And on the ſtubborn furrow dwell again.
Untainted with corruption's ſordid arts
The great man's virtues mend the peaſants' hearts ;
Stateſmen then ſhone true patriots at the helm,
And all were PITTS and Guardians of the realm.

Their boſoms, center'd in ſeverer care,
Left foreign lux'ry to its native air ;
They left the ſcaly breed th' unenvy'd ſeas,
In wanton aukwardneſs to ſport at eaſe ;
They left the dolphins, an unwieldy train,
To flounce in floods, and gambol thro' the main ;
To minuets thus grown gentlemen advance,
True dolphins taught by Duke and Hart to dance.

                                              Round

Round the rais'd maypole, on the velvet mead,
The ruſtic train the feſtal tranſports lead;
Smiles from the harmleſs fair the mirth improv'd,
Alike each neighbor loving, and belov'd.
The maſter's ſelf, unſkill'd with poliſh'd grace
Voters to bribe, or elbow for a place,
With no French fopp'ries fir'd his dazzled view,
Plain Engliſh ſounds, and thoſe alone he knew.
The plate ſecure within the ſpacious hall
No pilf'rer dreads, tho' open'd wide to all;
Each honeſt heart contented with his own
Ey'd not another's with a longing groan:
View, Britons, view—with ſhouts of envy praiſe
The golden bleſſings of thoſe halcyon days.

With gen'rous ardor th' uncorrupted train
Pour'd their devotions at religion's fane;
With ſtep ſpontaneous duty's path they trod,
No earthquake's horrors egg'd them to their God;
'Gainſt no invaſion's threats their vows they ſtay,
But ev'ry ſabbath's a thankſgiving-day.

Yes, thus were Britons bleſs'd, ere ſlaves to gold,
For pay their hearts and liberty they ſold;
When lib'ral grandeur's well-frequented door
Reliev'd the helpleſs, and oblig'd the poor;
When to full age the tow'ring timber ſpread,
Nor for a debt of honor bow'd the head.

M 2

With

With high ambition modern nobles glow,
Their food, their raiment not for ufe but fhew;
The friendly treat quite fick'ning they behold,
Like Midas wifhing all they touch'd was gold;
Infipid charms the plenteous boards difpenfe,
Unlefs the room is furnifh'd with expence.
Can SUCH on honeft Englifh lux'ry dine,
Content without a fmack of foreign wine?
While taftelefs artifices cloud their treat,
Such whims fantaftic, that you cannot eat!
And ftructures huge, with vulgar fweetmeats ftor'd,
Burlefque Britannia's conquefts on the board.
Take then your vanities, ye flaves of wealth,
To none I make a facrifice of health;
And time, that treafure I to friends devote,
Slow lags with dullnefs in th' embroider'd coat.

The high-born gueft let folly's vot'ries own,
Who meafure others by themfelves alone;
Fond in a toy, a bauble to delight,
Who feek a dinner but to pleafe their fight.
Not fuch be mine; I promife grateful cheer,
Tho' not a fweet of foreign lux'ry here;
Tho' not an ortolan adorn my board,
No bird like this my little fields afford;
My treat no ufelefs ornaments fupply,
No filver decks it, for the tax runs high.

Let

Let the rich board of vanity impart
The keen vibrations of the carver's art;
No need of lectures for the focial treat,
To point the grand anatomy of meat;
While fifh, flefh, fowl, in parcel'd order lie,
And with a new-made fcience feaft the eye.
HERE welcome friends may mangle as they will,
Nor fear my cenfure, if they take their fill.

One thing, my friend, your cautious thought demands,
No word of French poor Jofeph underftands;
Neat in attire the decent flaves fhall fhine,
Fear not thy purfe, th' unliv'ry'd is not mine;
My vaffals two,—of late my grandfire's one,
The next a youth, a trufty tenant's fon.
With modeft look the ftripling takes his ftand,
Fix'd and obedient to his lord's command:
Were birth's high honors mine, my juft applaufe
Might feem the product of a fonder caufe.

Good gen'rous port will crown your Englifh tafte;
With this and raifin is my table grac'd;
Th' unwholfome draughts of France I dare not take,
The trafh defpifing for its nation's fake.

Nor think at Florio's board the tender maid
Will fhine in fafhion's purpled charms difplay'd;

M 3   Think

Think not inebriate tumult's ſtrain t' employ,
Tumult, the mimicry of feſtal joy:
Alas! no ſhameleſs ſcene thoſe eyes will ſee,—
Such modiſh fancies are too great for me.
Fancies well ſuited to the reſtleſs ſouls,
Whoſe frugal riot reaſon's voice controls;
Giant Hibernians, who uſurp renown,
And in the town's defence affront the town;
Who doat on handbills which they ſcarce can ſign,
And owe their reputation to their wine.
Should meaner mortals court each modiſh vice,
Debauch the virgin, or adore the dice,
Contempt and ſcorn their ſordid lot await;
Thoſe crimes with us are virtues with the GREAT.

Far diff'rent paſtime decks my rural feaſts,
The good my converſe, and the learn'd my gueſts;
But vainly here the flimſy taſte will call
For the loud, rumbling bluſter of Fingal;
Whoſe tip-toe periods, SQUIRTED out, not SUNG,
Are ſcriptural, homeric, old and young,
Are any thing; tho', read it as you will,
Dear nonſenſe is at top and bottom ſtill.

And now, my friend, let reaſon's joys divert
Each weight of ſorrow harbor'd in thy heart;
Fell uſ'ry's pois'nous arts let others ſhare,
To others leave the money-jobbing care;

Nor ruthlefs jealoufy thy reft control,
For Cloe ftill, ftill loves thee to the foul.
And chief (or mirth is vain) refolv'd fufpend
The thanklefs anguifh for the trait'rous friend;
Be theirs alone the forrow who betray;
But—hence reflection to a future day.

Let the gay vot'ries of the graffy fport
To fam'd Newmarket's wide-ftretch'd plains refort;
Where buftling glow the rivals of the race,
With eager cries, the jockey and his grace;
And Nugax chief, who for the debt unpaid
Rais'd to the noble's arms the filial maid.
For thefe unpeopled London's glory fhrinks,
Ev'n England's felf in dear Newmarket finks;
While tow'rs the champion's heart of jockies fitft
To reign applauded, and of men the worft.

Hail, lovely paftime! great Newmarket, hail!
When once thy fports to fons of grandeur fail,
Then low'rs our country, with difhonor view'd,
As all her Indies were by France fubdu'd.
Thus England judges, her enthufiaft eyes
Hail modifh meannefs, and purfue with cries;
There wooe the maid, who fpreads her wanton airs
To footh with love the lofing gamefter's cares.

Yet

Yet ſtill, thou trifler, taſte th' unbounded play,
Go, reel from taverns at the noon of day,
Unknowing of a bluſh, in lordly ſtate,
And meet perhaps a parent at the gate ;
Then own, vain prodigal of time and pelf,
Thou'rt ſick of life, of pleaſure, of thyſelf.
Tho' the breaſt revel in the ſweets of joy,
Yet laughter ſoon, ſoon droops, and pleaſures cloy ;
A glut of tranſport palls the liſtleſs heart,
The ſoul's diſhonor, and the body's ſmart.

THE

THE

TWELFTH SATIRE

IMITATED.

HAIL, happy morn! thrice hail thy genial ray,
Which ſhines ſuperior to my natal day!
To humbler joys thoſe moments I commend
Which gave me breath, than thoſe which gave a friend.

Hilario ſafe we'll ſeize the gentle fawn,
Which wanton ſports along the verdant lawn;
And harmleſs flits his little horns to prove
'Gainſt ev'ry bark that decks the tow'ring grove.
We'll take fair innocency's pride, the lamb,
That browſing ſkips around the fleecy dam;
Nor heed the tender mother's bleating cries,
Whoſe anxious ſteps purſue the raviſh'd prize.

Did

Did gracious Heav'n th' exalted pow'r afford,
Ev'n as my bofom lib'ral were my board ;
To diftant climes my reftlefs foul would fly,
Where Sol unweary'd fires the fultry fky ;
India her richeft turtle fhould provide,
Soon o'er my difh I'd fpread its various pride ;
Whofe fmoaking fweets the glories fhould explain
Which feaft the laughing fons of lux'ry's train :
But what tho' heaps on heaps my table grae'd ?
Alas ! true friendfhip lives not by the tafte.

Sincerer welcome long-loft friends demand,
Who, fav'd from danger, tread their native land ;
Who ftill in terror hear the billows roar,
And fhudd'ring wonder, they're fecure on fhore.
Reflection poring o'er her recent ills
Again the horrors of the tempeft feels ;
Again the thunders roar, the lightnings fly,
To fhew the midnight gloom that loads the fky ;
Repeated woes the lab'ring foul infpire,
A crackling cordage, and the fails on fire ;
With rage recruited fwells the whirling blaft,
All cry with groans, " This moment is our laft !"

If Maro's pen with animated art
In pictur'd force the tempeft's rage impart,
" While the huge waves in lifted mountains roll,
" And the loud thunder wheels from pole to pole ;"

If

If thus the mufe the fhudd'ring bofom fcare,
How heaves the doubled agony of care,
When circling horrors fink the confcious breaft,
Stript of cool fiction's imitative veft!

Such ills as thefe ev'n George's * bofom knew,
Whofe threat'ning danger fir'd his gen'rous crew;
When the tofs'd billows of the ftormy deep,
Unfooth'd by monarchs, fill the groaning fhip;
The paufing pilot chill'd by ruffling fears
Miftrufts his fkill, and trembles as he fteers.
The fons of grandeur toil to fave in vain
The gifts of lux'ry from the greedy main;
Each dear-bought labor of the foreign loom,
The gold's rich fplendor, and the purple's bloom,
(Whofe charms had elfe difplay'd their pow'rful art
To win fome dazzled virgin's love-fick heart)
No deep-fetch'd figh, no flowing tear can fave,
Forc'd undiftinguifh'd to the watry grave.

Now fink the treafur'd ftores, the rich-carv'd plate,
And ev'ry fplendid vanity of ftate;
In vain (for ALL th' infatiate waves demand)
Shine forth the living ftrokes of Raphael's hand;
In vain the goblet fheds its fparkling ftore,
Doom'd to th' exhaufting lip of mirth no more;

* Storm in 1736.

Tho'

Tho' rich as ought that Gallia's treach'rous train
From a brib'd German garrifon can gain.

Away, cries av'rice, 'mid the defp'rate ftrife,
Spare but my gold, I care not for my life;
Tho' danger frown, what madnefs fears for health,
When clofely circled by the fmiles of wealth:
More fordid finks the foul as treafures thrive,
And curs'd with hoarded plenty dares not live.
Now ufe, fad refuge, gives her ling'ring prize,
And ftill the tempeft beats, the dangers rife;
The lifted maft, fo deep of life the love,
They force impatient from its height above,
Defpair's laft dread refource; the lighten'd fhip
Winds on unguided o'er th' unfriendly deep.

Go then, vain main, as fav'rite folly calls,
Coop'd in a tott'ring prifon's wooden walls;
Go, urg'd by av'rice, obftinately blind,
Brave ev'ry danger of the fea and wind;
Sail on fecure; nor heed thy fleeting breath,
Scarce four fmall inches from the gates of death;
There 'mid the tempeft own, thy fordid care
Too great to plow the ocean of defpair.

But now at once the jarring tempefts ceafe,
The weary'd waves lie level'd into peace;

No more the wond'ring pilot droops aghaſt,
A zephyr-breeze controls the Northern blaſt :
The ſhip in ſails of vary'd colors dreſs'd,
Torn from the toiling ſailors' dropping veſt,
Glides o'er the main ; while Phœbus' beamy head.
O'er Heav'n's pure azure pours his ſmiling red.

Now full to view the wiſh'd-for plains appear,
Whoſe cliffs on high their whiten'd glories rear ;
With eager cries they hail the welcome land,
And Albion, Albion ecchoes to the ſtrand ;
Urg'd on triumphant with a proſp'rous gale,
To Dover's friendly ſmiles they ſwell their ſail.
Hail, happy ſeat ! by nature's hand diſplay'd,
Inviting refuge to the ſoul of trade !
Stand and admire her tutelary charms,
Ye ſhiv'ring ſailors, foſter'd in her arms.
Lo ! now with tears of joy your ſpouſes meet,
And their lov'd lords with fond embraces greet ;
Pant ev'ry ſecret of the ſtorm to know,
And hang devouring on the tale of woe.

Haſte then, my friends, the genial ſtrain prepare,
Revel in bliſs, and bid adieu to care ;
Let ſparkling tranſports crown the feſtal bowl,
And muſic's ſofter treaſures ſooth the ſoul ;
I too the gen'ral voice of mirth will join,
And richeſt incenſe ſhow'r on friendſhip's ſhrine ;

Yes,

Yes, my full arms each living flow'r shall bring,
O'er nature scatter'd from the hand of spring;
The vi'let's variegated sweets disclose,
The paler lily, and the blooming rose :
When Phœbus sinks beneath the veil of night,
The jovial dance shall close the gay delight.

Nor think that ought but friendship's pow'rful claim
Lights in my lifted soul this ardent flame ; .
Think not my wishes from Hilario wait
Some kind encreases to a small estate ;
Three healthy babes such fond desires annoy,
The sweet memorials of the nuptial joy;
And sure 'twere vain with lib'ral arm to send
Frail expectation's gifts to such a friend.

If fell disease Avaro's limbs oppress,
Each hour the cringing supplicants addrefs ;
With many a sob they squeeze the tear-less eye,
And tire with ceaseless pray'r the cruel sky.
" With joy," cries Florio, " I'd refign my breath,
" Thus could I save my dearest lord from death ;
" To lift the good man from the bed of pain
" Would fly each soothing remedy to gain ;
" Did distant realms the healing draught afford,
" I'd search content to place it on thy board ;
" At friendship's nod with conscious joy would tread
" The frozen desart, or the scorching mead ;
" 'Mid

" 'Mid the loud din of India's favage arms
" I'd wander, carelefs of the war's alarms;
" With face unmov'd the fcene of flaughter fee,
" Unknown to fear, for fuch a friend as thee."

So roar the fycophants with fervent will,
Wretches from fhew of kindnefs bent to kill:
When thus againft him friends and phyfic ftrive,
How great the wonder if he 'fcape alive !

Some dare devote, to fave his dearer life,
The kind domeftic, or the faithful wife;
Tho' beauty's charms with heav'nly luftre bloom,
Thofe lovely charms they offer to the tomb;
Bind with paternal hand their only boy,
And at the ftake difplay the fav'rite joy;
Not, like the facred monarch, doom'd to find,
Their Ifaac to redeem, a captive hind.

Far purer friendfhip crowns my focial plan,
I fpurn the riches, but I prize the man;
And know, thou flatt'rer, fhould the fon of wealth
With limbs recruited tread the bow'rs of health,
The fiend congenial may refign his pelf
To fome low cringer, worthlefs as thyfelf;
Whofe tow'ring foul (unrival'd blifs !) will reign,
And give to thee to murmur and complain.

Still

Still curs'd with age let menial vaſſals live,
And the long triumphs of the oak ſurvive ;
Heap in th' extended cheſt the glitt'ring ſtore,
And ſtill contentleſs, ever groan for more ;
Their haughty fronts like brutal Jeff'ries rear,
Scoff at the widow's cry, and orphan's tear ;
Yet—poor the tranſports of the guilty breaſt,
The world deteſting—whom the world deteſt.

THE

THIRTEENTH SATIRE

IMITATED.

NO more, I pray, no more—the daring foul,
 Whofe impious fteps the paths of fin control,
 Confcience will fting; no charms can footh to reft
 The troubled ocean of a guilty breaft;
Nor fuch with patient eye can juftice fee,
Tho' clear'd his conduct by the court's decree.
Tho' bafe corruption ftop the arm of right,
The fmile of int'reft, or the frown of might,
Lone fits the wretch from focial converfe hurl'd,
Difdain'd he pines, the refufe of the world.

 Away, thefe mournful ftrains, thefe murm'ring cries!
Such trivial ills demand th' unmanly fighs?
N   A me-

A menial pilf'rer vex his ruffled hours,
Whom heav'n has loaded with her choiceſt ſtores?
Pauſe from thy grief; the circling world ſurvey
What hapleſs numbers ſink to fraud a prey!
Few are the bleſs'd, whoſe ſky with ſmile ſerene
Gilds the fair morn, and cloudleſs ſhuts the ſcene.
The ſtorm the great man views with patient eyes,
Nor ſwells his ſorrow, but as dangers riſe;
What! injur'd friendſhip mourn? know, falſhood's crimes
Are but the fainteſt image of the times;
So rare the juſt, whoſe careleſs looks behold
A neighbor's treaſure, and diſdain the gold;
Rare in theſe times, which harden'd knav'ry feed,
Rare as the Scotſmen left beyond the Tweed.

In vain has age, if vice thy boſom ſcare,
With hoary wiſdom ſilver'd o'er thy hair;
Wiſdom to threeſcore honeſt winters known,
When northern Galba GUIDES the Britiſh th—e.
In vain experience crowns thy thoughtful mind,
Which wond'ring views the manners of mankind.

With ſtudy'd force let grave divines diſpenſe
The ſober truths of moral eloquence,
And loudly fierce the pulpit leſſons give,
(Not from their own examples) how to live;
Far greater they, whoſe uncorrupted heart
From action's ſelf the precept can impart;

Who,

Who, when misfortune fhow'rs th' afflictive pain,
Smile at its rage, and fpurn th' oppreffing chain.

What place fo facred damps the murd'rer's foul!
What fabbath checks the fury of the bowl!
Religion's walks here daring footfteps fpoil;
Here roars th' undaunted atheift's madden'd toil.
Thin-fcatter'd fteps to virtue's fane refort,
How poor her kingdom, and how mean her court!
See, how fhe treads with falt'ring terror flow,
Scoff'd and infulted by the haughty foe!
What brand, what ftamps of infamy fuffice
To mark this age of complicated vice!

Yet—ftill does Titus with impetuous flame
Still madly fervent, as the herd, exclaim,
Who fawning o'er a noble's fulfome joke
Expectant hang, and grin before 'tis fpoke?
Still call in curfes to the confcious fky,
To blaft the perjur'd, and revenge his cry?
Grey in thy years, but infant in thy thought,
Thy harmlefs foul what poor experience taught!
What folly told thee, that the fplendid prize
Would fpread in vain its charms to human eyes?
Believe me, friend, the world with fmiles will find
This patriarch-rudenefs of thy fpotlefs mind.

Such, fuch was man, when Harold's golden reign
Spread richeft bleffings o'er Britannia's plain;

Ere

Ere Norman tyranny's impetuous arm
Fill'd the wide realm with terror and alarm;
And proudly ſtalking to th' inhuman fight
The ſceptre wreſted from the hand of right.
Then glow'd the monarch's breaſt with patriot-zeal,
He liv'd true guardian of the public weal;
Not ſkill'd to proſtitute the gifts of ſtate,
He ſmil'd, and bad the good man to be great.
No wanton fair improv'd the courtly feaſt,
But welcom'd virtue ſhone a conſtant gueſt;
ALL ſhar'd the princely grace; no rigid wall
Coop'd the dread ſovereign from his people's call;
No party-frenzy ſhook the ſolid throne,
The Whig alike, and Tory then unknown;
No thankleſs courtier daring inſults ſpread,
And rak'd the aſhes of the royal dead;
None on a WILLIAM's triumphs learn'd to ſneer,
To feed with flatt'ry's ſtrain an ANNA's ear.
Nor then did faſhion's awful pow'r begin
To ſmile on folly, or to varniſh ſin;
With manly reverence youth's corruptleſs age
Paid ſacred honors to the bearded ſage;
Superior riches were a vain pretence
In pamper'd dullneſs to ſuperior ſenſe;
Inſtructive wiſdom thro' the realm was priz'd,
Not ſneer'd by ſtriplings, and as now deſpis'd.

When

When juſtice greets me with her fainteſt rays,
I view this queen of virtues with amaze,
That honeſt goodneſs meets a friendly place,
A corner in the heart of human race.

Soon ſhall I hope to hear the Ruſſian's tongue
Active to ſentence ought, but what is wrong;
Soon ſhall I hope Germania's ſons to ſee
Cloth'd in the garb of meek humility;
That haughty Spain referve's cold arts will ceaſe,
Nor with ſuſpicions damp the ſmile of peace:
Spain whoſe rich ſtores in ceaſeleſs channels flow,
And the low frauds of forward knav'ry ſhew.
Away; nor ſtill thy trivial loſs deplore;
I'd thank MY GUARDIAN, had he ſtoln no more;
Cheerful wou'd thank him, and pronounce it juſt
To pare ſome uſual perquiſites of truſt;
Ev'n hireling agents from the plenteous cheſt
Should ſhare the gleanings, did they ſave the reſt.

Mark how yon wretch the ſacred ſtrain diſplays,
How dwells with rapture on religion's praiſe!
Each conſcious thought with gen'rous freedom glows;
Serenely bold th' exalted period flows;
" To thee, juſt heav'n, my ſpotleſs vows I ſend,
" To thee, whom injur'd virtue calls her friend;
" If perjury's mine, eternal ſtains diſgrace,
" Eternal curſes blaſt my guilty race;

N 3

" If perjury's mine, celeftial vengeance fall,
" Deftruction crufh my fon, my wife, and ALL ›
" To join the heap this worthlefs bleffing throw,
" To groan with Satan in the realms below."

Some think, that influenc'd by the nod of chance,
The fpheres leap'd forth to form the heav'nly dance;
And boldly carelefs of the pow'r above,
Sneer at his goodnefs, and difdain his love.
Some calmly cautious quit the paths of right,
Their fouls ftart doubtful with a wild affright;
Point but the gold, no more the ling'rers ftay,
But rufh rapacious of the fplendid prey.

Had heav'n but proffer'd one poor fhilling more
T' increafe the hoarded loads of Lowther's ftore,
Each ill the wretch with tranfport had endur'd,
The fons of medicine ever gave or cur'd,
" In never-fading bloom let others fhine,
" Torture I heed thee not—fo wealth be mine."

Tho' num'rous crimes celeftial wrath provoke,
Th' indulgent pow'r ftands paufing o'er the ftroke;
On wings of rage tho' blazing lightnings fly,
And thunders roar the frown divine on high;
Still tow'rs my foul in confcious boldnefs free,
No errors from the world diftinguifh me.

There

There are, whofe'crimes in glaring horrors glow,
Whofe meek repentance wards th' impending blow;
There are, whofe triumphs fire their guilty breaft
As juftice for a while were lull'd to reft;
Rewards precarious load the lifted fcale,
This meets a r—b—d, and the next a jail.

Such flatt'ring ftrains a quick'ning fire impart,
Steel the rais'd foul, and petrify the heart;
Who firft ftand falt'ring on the ftormy fhore,
Launch to the main and ply the willing oar;
They rufh difdainful of th' Almighty rod,
With perjury loaded to their confcious God;
Survey the well-known name with carelefs eye,
Smile at the fignet, and the prize deny.

Why then fanatic zeal thy foul excite,
Like Wefley bawling to the fons of night?
Or wildly frantic, as the brother-block,
Who deals his pure reflections at the Lock?
" Lo! gracious heav'n, what impious deeds provoke
" Thy lifted vengeance, and defy the ftroke!
" Hark! the loud cries of injur'd truth require,
" Quick fnatch thy dreadful minifters of ire;
" Devote the victim for the world a fign,
" A blafted monument of wrath divine;
" Elfe whence fhould man thy fovereign goodnefs own?
" Whence court the fmile of heav'n, or fear the frown?

" Nor

" Nor hear the tempefts of Almighty rage,
" Calm as the mimic thunder of the ftage?"

Yet give the mufe, my Titus, to control
With foothing voice the fervor of thy foul;
The moral thought no wild ROMAINE infpires,
Pure are my dictates from th' enthufiaft's fires;
Ill fuits with friendfhip's tongue the ranting ftrain,
That fcares the reafon of the vulgar train:
Nor claim THESE evils phyfic's formal tribe,
Not all the college can a cure prefcribe.

Look round the world, and if another's breaft
Groan not with fortune's heavier ills opprefs'd,
Feed the deep forrow, give a loofe to care,
Heave the full groan, nor check the flowing tear;
Wrap'd in the fable weeds of grief deplore,
And clofe to comfort's call thy rigid door;
With ling'ring folemn ftep demurely tread,
As at the funeral of the friendly dead;
Loft gold demands no cold diffembled fighs,
A weight of woe beft fuits the ravifh'd prize;
Not fuch as theirs, whofe fympathizing breaft
Howls the forc'd ftrain, and tears the fhatter'd veft.

The daring fouls of our degen'rate times
Are fpotted thick with deeper ftains of crimes;

Difclaim

Difclaim the writing, tho' the perjury ftare,
Hideous to view, and fpeak with frowning glare.
But thou, whofe high-exalted ftation grace
The glow of riches, and the pomp of race,
Think'ft not an ill fhou'd ftain thy honor'd birth,
A weight form'd only for the fcum of earth.

Alas! in vain with unrelenting ire
You launch 'gainft perjury the raging fire,
Here on the trav'ler's gold the pilf'rer preys,
Here murd'rers fpread the city in a blaze;
In vain his walls the flumb'ring rich immure,
No midnight's gloom his quiet can fecure;
From felon hands no church its gold can fave;
In vain the dead lie bofom'd in the grave;
Forth roam the wretches, and indignant wreft
The clay-cold reliques from their bed of reft;
While daring thoughts ev'n rev'rend avarice move
To tear his Savior from the height above.

See for his fire the fon's impetuous foul
With impious venom tips the fmiling bowl;
Cuts the thin mould'ring thread of ling'ring breath,
And fnatches from the fates the work of death:
No equal pangs such defp'rate breafts can feel,
The rack too gentle, and too mild the wheel.

Yet,

Yet, would my Titus count the crouded crimes,
That ſtamp the buſy genius of the times,
Hence to the court, the courſe of juſtice ſee,
Then own, that others live more curs'd than thee;
Such there the ſins (ſtrange pow'r!) with frighten'd gaze
The jury ſhudd'ring, and the judge ſurveys.

Lives there, who views with wonder's ſtarting eye
Falſe Holland burſt the bands of amity,
With parlying inſult fir'd by pride advance
The bulky ſlave of dulneſs and of France?
Degen'rate from their ſires, a warlike hoſt
When their own William rul'd the Engliſh coaſt.
—Yet, England ſtill be free, their threats diſdain;
Nor ſooth with fondling notes a DASTARD train.

When haughty Gallia arms her bugbear hoſt,
And num'rous ſquadrons crowd the hoſtil coaſt,
Impatient fame on haſty pinions bears
The low'ring vengeance to the Britiſh ears.
Of old, 'tis true, this dread parade of might
Might chill the vulgar and the great affright;
Now the calm reaſon unbelieving ſmiles
On the mock frenzy, and diſdains their toils.

" Shall ſplendid wealth the guilty boſom guard?
" Shall, gracious heav'n, the perjur'd meet reward?"

Yet

Yet feize the captive, would thy barbarous pow'r
With torment load his life's remaining hour?
Yes, o'er the rack th' extended limbs difplay,
The much-mourn'd debt can cruelty repay!
How poor the heart with mercy's fweets unblefs'd!
How mean the deed, where vengeance fires the breaft!

   'Tis true—the crowd with fouls rapacious pour
The ftorms of rage, and loofe the vengeful fhow'r;
Unthinking crew! how vain the frenzy fhewn,
To gild the caufe, which juftice calls her own.
Far diff'rent fhines the martyr's heav'nly pride
Who liv'd in virtue, and in virtue dy'd;
Far different fhines in life's defpondent day
The * Queen whofe ruin was a father's fway.
Celeftial fair! in native fplendor great
She fpurn'd the tinfel of a regal ftate;
And round in blazing pageantry difplay'd
Pants for the quiet of the rural fhade.
Yes, when the † tyrant gave the fatal blow,
No curfes blafted her exalted foe;
Not her's revenge, which loads ungen'rous tongues,
Not her's a figh but for her country's wrongs.

   Is't not enough that gnawing confcience fpreads
Her whips and fcorpions o'er the vicious heads;

* Lady Jane Grey.   † Mary.

Can

Can deeper pangs await the flave of fin,
Where guilt's oppreffion fills the mind within?
Guilt, confcious guilt, with never-ceafing fright
Fills the fad day, and loads the fleeplefs night;
Bids ev'ry crime with double fury glare,
And racks the foul with horror and defpair.

Of old with giddy breaft a youthful lord
Gave to his fteward's truft a fecret hoard;
With hiring charms the high-pil'd treafure fhone,
Horatio figh'd, and wifh'd it for his own;
Yet ling'ring doubted, ere he fnatch'd the prize,
And firft to heav'n extends his wifhful eyes.
" While dreary evils load my abject ftate,
" Siege my fad hours, and crowd my humble gate,
" Forgive me, heav'n, if poverty furvey
" With many a longing look the fplendid prey.
" Yet fhou'd I take (unlefs thy pow'r defend,
" I dare not harm my mafter, and my friend)
" Is juftice mine?" at this with dread alarm
The thunder's roar draws back th' uplifted arm;
The fudden fhock his confcious bofom fires,
The cheft he quits, and checks his fond defires.

Would others thus with virtue's precepts fraught
Paufe, ere to deeds they fwell th' ungen'rous thought,
Would others thus, whofe bofoms' wayward will
Warps from fair truth, and feeds a wifh of ill,

2   Ponder

Ponder the crime, what agonizing darts
Would turn their fury, and efcape their hearts!

The ceafelefs forrows of the guilty foul
No reft can footh, no pleafure can control;
In vain the board exhales its fmoaking ftores,
In vain her fweets celeftial mufic pours;
Loft in defpair he mourns his abject fate,
Like Wolfey blafted by the frown of ftate;
Whofe lips with fervor fhow'r'd at Henry's nod
Thofe pray'rs, he never offer'd to his God.

But for a while fhou'd raving anguifh ceafe,
And nature toil to momentary peace;
Infulted virtue ftalks before his fight,
And frowning fwells the tempeft of affright;
But chief my Titus' facred form appears,
Glares in his eyes, and thunders in his ears;
And fnatches from its cell each confcious fin,
That harbor'd fleeps, and loads the foul within.
See how he ftarts; each more than Zephyr-wind
Speaks the dread fury of th' Almighty mind;
And ere a cloud the blue ferene deform,
Scar'd he lies fhudd'ring at th' expected ftorm;
Not all its crimes to guilt appall'd can yield
'Gainft hoftil confcience a protective fhield.
No more the lightning's flafh at random thrown,
Aim'd at no other's crimes, but his alone;

Now

Now the hufh'd tempeft fooths the torture's pain;
The Zephyrs whifper, and he raves again ;
Tho' vengeance fleep, when crimes its rage provoke,
'Tis but to add frefh vigor to the ftroke.

If dire difeafes fhake his lab'ring frame,
The gout's fwoln anguifh, or the fever's flame;
How fierce the pangs ! th' Almighty finger glows
In ev'ry limb, and fills th' augmented woes;
With horror funk the wretch devoted lies,
Nor dares one vow to footh the angry fkies;
In life's laft gafp he drags his ling'ring breath,
And groans for refuge from the arm of death :
Say, earth, what evils o'er thy kingdoms reign,
Sharp as the dying finner's galling pain ?

Who treads the flow'ry bow'rs, the verdant mead,
To realms of vice whofe luring traces lead,
Trips fmoothly headlong with unguarded mind,
Nor heeds the call of virtue from behind.
With ling'ring fteps the pond'ring feet begin,
But foon fly wifhful to the fmile of fin ;
In cloudlefs fkies they fee no tempeft low'r
Beyond th' horizon of the prefent hour.

Yet weep no more, with profp'rous crimes elate
The daring villain but provokes his fate;

Know,

Know, heav'n's Almighty pow'r with paufing thought
Weighs ev'ry deed, and numbers ev'ry fault;
Th' uplifted arm will drop the ftroke at laft,
And loaded with their crimes the guilty blaft.
See, fnatch'd at once to India's diftant plains
Groans the fcorch'd wretch in flav'ry's galling chains;
Or life's thin dregs with flowly-ling'ring doom
Pine 'midft the horrors of a dungeon's gloom;
Hence then, my friend, thefe melancholy cries,
Feed with his tears, and triumph in his fighs;
And own, that juftice heav'nly wrath infpires,
Calls down its thunders, and directs its fires.

THE

THE

FOURTEENTH SATIRE

IMITATED.

TRUE, there are crimes, my friend, whofe pois'nous
   art
  Taints the fair beauties of the virtuous heart ;
Crimes, which diftinguifh'd in the father run
Thro' one continued line from fon to fon.
See Clodio tow'ring on Newmarket's plain
Plies the loud lafh, and joins the Jockey train ;
While bold behind him, with a rival grace,
His hopeful offspring glories in the race ;
Scours the wide champain with a gen'rous fire,
And bawls out oaths as roughly as the fire.

Mark

Mark too Hilario, whofe unbounded foul
With ceafelefs tranfport drains the fparkling bowl ;
And hanging fondly on a prattling lord,
Grins conftant gueft at his luxurious board ;
Whofe menial hands each labor'd difh attend,
To pleafe the palate of his noble friend.
Then fee the fon, nor teftify furprize,
Who fcarce has ceas'd the cradle's infant cries ;
In vain the dictates of the bearded fage
Point wifdom's precept to his tender age ;
Still, like the father, a rapacious gueft,
He courts the treafures of the gaudy feaft ;
Still does the board's luxurious fmile purfue,
And fnuffs the incenfe with a longing view.

Can vengeful Richard, whofe impetuous will
The bloody fcenes of favage flaughter fill,
Whofe ruthlefs finger ties the fatal cord,
And to the wife difplays the flaughter'd lord,
And fondly rev'ling in inhuman joys
Strips of their infant-lives the kindred boys ;
Can HE the harmlefs fouls of youth improve
With the mild thoughts of clemency and love ?
Who views the fubject train with frowns of fcorn,
And thinks for kings alone the world was born ?

Influenc'd alas ! by nature's pow'rful tie
We view a parent's deeds with longing eye ;

Ev'n glaring faults in virtue's form appear,
When taught by thofe whom infants we revere.
There are, 'tis true, whom nature's hands difplay,
Severely model'd from a purer clay,
Who boldly leap the bounds of kindred birth,
And tread the paths of reafon, and of worth.
The herd ftill chain'd to the paternal lore
Heed but the fteps their fathers trod before;
Fly then from evil with affrighted pace,
Left the track'd failure blacken all thy race ;
Too foon we're won by fin's enchanting ftrain,
While worth oft beckons to her fhrine in vain.
Yes, lodg'd in ev'ry clime, in ev'ry realm,
We fee fome Steuart tow'ring at the helm ;
A virtuous George but rarely decks the throne,
Indulg'd by Heav'n to Britain's ftate alone.

Far from the bounds of thy corruptlefs cell
Drive ev'ry vice, and ev'ry crime expel;
No fcene of ill to infant eyes appear,
Or footh with tickling plume the ravifh'd ear :
Tremble, ye fires, when thoughts impure ye feed,
And think your offspring views th' ungen'rous deed.
For fhould his bofom's future acts demand
Th' avenging ftroke of law's correcting hand,
From THEE alone th' inglorious actions glare,
Thy want of virtue, or thy want of care.

O 2   Know

Know 'tis thy tafk, by heav'nly pow'r affign'd,
To form at once his body and his mind;
From THEE the fwelling buds of ill require
Perfuafion's foftnefs, or the voice of ire.

But whence the free-born licence to control
The crimes and errors of the youthful foul?
Whence the wife precepts' angry founds impart,
When blacker actions blot thy vicious heart?
Retire; nor more the healthful med'cines yield
To others' madnefs till thyfelf art heal'd.

Yet fee, when friendfhip's journeying footfteps wait,
With fmile invited at thy well-known gate,
See! on each fide thy fummon'd vaffals fly;
Difplay the fideboard forth, with rage you cry;
Quick cleanfe the plate, and ope the drawing-room;
Hence to your bufinefs, for my lord is come:
Whence yon black cobweb, whence this fpotted floor?
—Let all be neatnefs, or you're mine no more.

And does Licinius thus with anxious fears
Storm in confufion when a friend appears?
What fhudder to be feen, but richly drefs'd
In a poor finery's encumb'ring veft?
Difplay thy blooming fon in gay attire,
With glitt'ring outfide, worthy of his fire?

Nor

Nor heed the wrinkles and the fpots of fin,
Which fpread contagion on the foul within?

Go, bid the youth in gen'rous virtue fhine,
Thy country thanks thee, and applaufe is thine;
Bid him the pondrous arms of glory wield,
And rufh for truth and Britain to the field;
When honor calls, the jarring founds to ceafe,
And to the world reftore the fweets of peace:
Thus bid him act; when virtue meets his eyes,
Her charms the ftripling dares not to defpife.

See how the parent-ftorks with rapid wing
Launch o'er the field, and on the ferpent fpring;
Or bear in tranfport to their wifhful train
The lizard chirping on the verdant plain!
But fiercer far the vulture's rav'nous breaft,
To ftill the clamors of her craving neft;
With headlong rage fhe rufhes from on high,
Where the huge oxens' filthy relics lie;
Or where the gallows' loaded arms are fpread
With the bafe corfes of th' ignoble dead;
Then haftes away, and feafts her favage brood,
Who mangling riot in the barb'rous food.

The free-born eagle thro' the realms of air
With darting fury foufes on the hare,

O'ertakes

O'ertakes the swifter kidling's rapid feet,
And snatches from the plain the gen'rous treat ;
The tender eaglet, arm'd with strengthen'd force,
Now tow'rs embolden'd his aspiring course,
Flies forth provok'd by hunger's keen desire,
And snaps the victim with the parent's fire.

Sir Visto, seiz'd with building's fatal rage,
In splendid structures feeds his riper age ;
To Dorset's plains his eager wishes fly ;
In stately pride he rears the dome on high.
The columns tow'r magnificently great,
But scarce o'erlook an acre of estate :
And oh ! the taste life's precious hours to drown,
Wrap'd in the country—what ! forsake the town?
Thus sings the demon lux'ry in his ear,
He seeks the glories of the spacious square ;
There the rich structure swells on ev'ry side,
Huge as unwieldy Blenheim's dazzling pride ;
There the proud lordling o'er the wealthy race
He struts and spurns each mortal—like his grace.

Tho' rapt'rous joy for some short moments reign'd,
The streaming fountain must at length be drain'd ;
Thus Visto sinks by poverty deprefs'd,
His works a laughter, and himself a jest.
Should frenzy fire his offspring to pursue
Th' exalted grandeur that Sir Visto knew,

How

How would the vice congenial tow'ring rife,
And with example's influ'nce ftrike the eyes !

Th' uncomely Jew, whofe fuperftitious law
Keeps ev'ry Sabbath with religious awe,
Studious to cloke of wealth th' ungen'rous care,
Who tires the fynagogue with fervent pray'r,
Nor dares to fhed the fwine's much-honor'd flood,
But fucks in greedy vengeance human blood ;
The Roman, center'd in himfelf alone,
Each fect with curfes fpurning but his own,
Stiffly pronouncing all repentance vain,
Till holy water fanctify the brain,
Who counting beads on beads demurely ftands,
And hugs his gods of clay with frantic hands,
Each has his faults ; his glaring errors fhine
From fire to fon in one continued line.

'Tis true, tho' other fins they thoughtlefs prize,
Yet av'rice knows no charms in youthful eyes ;
Not like the fire they hug the fplendid prey ;
Give but the treafure, and it flies away.
In vain the fathers point the folly dreft
In meek frugality's feverer veft ;
In vain the fober precept they impart,
So loathing to a gay afpiring heart.

" Is't

" Is't then a crime the treasure to defend
" Which snatches in its flight each worldly friend ;
" Or guard with fonder arms from hostil hate
" Than Gallia's sons the tyrant of their state ?
" Besides—the world with eager tongue proclaim
" The rich man's glories to the height of fame ;
" The toils of virtuous industry display,
" Amassing careful for the future day.
" Survey the wealthy, how his soul employs
" Life's blissful moments in serenest joys !
" No galling cares, which with the poor man dwell,
" And blot the quiet of the straw-roof'd cell."

On then, bold youth ; the bright example view,
With rival step the heav'nly track pursue ;
Wealth, wealth alone will man's applauses draw,
And keep the slanders of the world in awe.
The soul first conscious of the crime within
Just steps and pilfers in the mire of sin ;
But soon impatient slacks th' unguided rein,
And stretches headlong on the field of gain.
Behold thin morsels scatter'd o'er his board,
While pale and meagre frowns the wealthy lord ;
Behold the vassals like Avaro fed
With scarce a scanty scrap of moulder'd bread,
Bear at his nod the poor remains away,
The precious substance of a future day ;

To

To fuch the mendicant with famine worn
Would grudge acceptance, and with horror fcorn.
If by board-wages nourifh'd (happier lot !)
With poring eye he pries into the pot;
Seeks from the fervants' fare to be fupply'd,
Nor dares a dinner for himfelf provide.

But whence this anxious toil, thefe ceafelefs fighs,
To rake in ufelefs hoards the glitt'ring prize ?
Know, ye vain wretches of rapacious foul,
Still rifes av'rice as the treafures roll;
Life's humbler courfe in ftreams of rapture flows,
It feeks no treafure, and no forrow knows.

Come then, with tow'ring foul triumphant fly,
Court the rich tranfports of the rural fky;
From fcene to fcene with bufy ardor roam,
Where verdant acres crown th' exalted dome.
Yet hold ; at once th' afpiring wifhes end—
Go, view the villa of thy neighbor-friend;
Where plenteous timber loads the foreft round,
And yellow treafures deck the fmiling ground.
Yes—fell he muft, to clear the lucklefs nights
Which drain'd his fubftance at the den of Whites;
Go, blefs the luring charms of cards and dice,
'Tis yours, Avaro, if you name your price.
Play, pow'rful fiend, eluded by thy charms
How the gull'd foul flies fondly to thy arms !

Too

Too foon, alas! to curfe the fatal hour,
When firft fhe fell the victim of thy pow'r.

Be mine far rather, fwells th' infatiate note,
To pile my treafures in a threadbare coat,
Than hear the poor with fervent voice proclaim·
My num'rous virtues, and unfpotted fame ;
If ftill unblefs'd by Heav'n's Almighty hands
With the rich plenty of uncounted lands.

Fond fool, will gold the body's pangs divert,
Or light up tranfport in the broken heart ?
Will gold extend life's quick-departing breath,
Or ftop the fury of the arm of death ?
The tomb HE opes, alas! for wealth and birth,
With iron foul, as for the dregs of earth.

When the great martyr rul'd Britannia's helm,
And bold rebellion fhook the bleeding realm,
Infulting Cromwell led the fatal way,
And gave the portion'd land the foldiers' prey.
The forrowing mafter meets difdainful fmiles ;
While, with the harveft of another's toils,
Stalk the flufh'd fiends, who made a nation groan,
And rear'd a low-born vagrant to the throne.
From fide to fide the liv'ry'd minions fly,
Fix'd on the wifhes of the mafter's eye ;

Invited

Invited nobles crowd the founding door,
But to the peafants' footfteps known before;
The little infants, and the harmlefs wife,
Gaze up, and wonder at their change of life.

O gold accurs'd ! what blackeft crimes we fee,
Ambition's darling, from the love of thee ?
By thee with impious rage the kindred foul
Difplays at once the dagger and the bowl.
Fix'd to their object, reftiff of the chain,
With wild impatience rufh the fons of gain ;
Steel'd to the blufh of fhame, purfue their flight,
And look defiance to the frown of right.

Be yours, my fons, the royalifts exclaim,
To tread in innocence the vale of fame ;
Yours the pure raptures of the lowly cot,
Unknown to treafon, of the world forgot.
Take they the fields ;—difdain th' unmanly groan,
And plough content thofe acres, late your own.
Misfortune's frowns whofe fteady bofoms prove,
Ne'er mifs th' applauding fmiles of Heav'n above;
The cot's calm joys unmix'd with tempefts flow,
While grandeur leads but to the realms of woe.

'Twas thus the father pointed virtue's choice ;
But now how vary'd founds th' inftructive voice !

Whcu

When winter's icy finger loads the fkies,
At break of day rapacious Macer flies:
Up, up, thou fluggard, fleep's dull fetters break,
And in the gloom of law impatient rake;
Sweet profit calls, purfue th' inviting care,
In knowledge rife an Hardwick at the bar.
Hail, Britons, hail, whofe dauntlefs arms are hurl'd,
And fill each fubject-quarter of the world!,
I fee your conquefts curb with awful rein.
The frauds of France, and infolence of Spain;
You fnatch the lifted ftandards from their hand,
And Britain's banners float on ev'ry land;
Proceed, ye heroes, with unbounded rage,
And your wide triumphs be your food—in age.

Do you, my Titus, tread a fafer plain,
Thro' law's dark allies thrid the paths of gain;
Be yours to varnifh o'er the caufe of wrong,
Eluding juftice with a fupple tongue;
To wealth alone to ope the yielding door,
Deaf to th' oppreffions of the fee-lefs poor;
The orphan's ftores with grudging eye furvey,
And half the treafure ravifh for thy prey;
With victor-fcorn the threats of toil behold,—
So fweet, fo lovely are the charms of gold!
Still let experience, life's beft guide, impart
This golden precept ftamp'd upon thy heart;

" None

" None aſks what ſpring ſupplies the glitt'ring mine,
" 'Tis needleſs whence it roſe when wealth is thine."
Thus in life's earlier morn is childhood taught,
And ſuckles with its milk the prudent thought.

Yet hear, rapacious ſoul, the ſov'reign rule,
Drawn from the ſacred truths of wiſdom's ſchool ;
Whence this impatient rage of fond deſire ?
Too ſoon the ſon will emulate his ſire ;
Toil with redoubled zeal for ſordid pelf,
Richer alike, and baſer than thyſelf.
Tho' native goodneſs rule the YOUTHFUL will,
While thinly ſcatter'd riſe the ſeeds of ill,
Yet the roots faſten'd into ſtrength control
The deep receſſes of the RIPER ſoul.

Survey him, ſteel'd to ſhame his harden'd face,
Show'r forth the perjur'd lie with manly grace ;
With hand undaunted on the ſacred book,
Center'd he ſtands in innocency's look.
Should Heav'n's indulgence give the beauteous wife,
That beauty's hateful bloom devotes her life ;
Black av'rice leering eyes the plenteous dow'r,
And haſtes the poiſon for the nuptial hour ;
With rapid ſtride ſtill panting for the gain
The earth ſhe ranſacks, and ſhe rakes the main.

Fondly

Fondly. the fon beholds the wand'ring fire,
His influence fteels him, and examples fire ;
When firft Avaro feeks the fplendid prey,
His child he beckons to the flipp'ry way ;
Whofe headlong courfe purfues the giddy plan,
The track once beat, reftrain him if you can.

Firft foft indulgence feeds th' ungen'rous thought,
At length to bolder action fwells the fault ;
Upbraid the heart, whofe bounty dares defend
From pining indigence the virtuous friend,
Strait av'rice ftains thy fon, with patient eyes
He'll view affliction, and difdain its cries.
Fix'd on this god his fanguin wifh will tow'r
Like Galba bafking in the glare of pow'r,
Whofe native art allures preferment's fmile
To gild the barren corner of an ifle ;
Hackney'd in menial toil, yet ftung by pride,
Where felfifh upftarts are to Heav'n ally'd ;
Who flaves of fraud, and to rebellion prone,
Deem all barbarians but themfelves alone.

Yet know, this ruthlefs lion after pelf
Will tear alike thy neighbor and thyfelf ;
Then wifh in vain to check the tow'ring fire,
Whofe fury fprings from madnefs of the fire.
Afk but thy heart, can greedy av'rice ftay
Till ling'ring nature clofe thy aged day ?

The filial hand will hafte the parting groan,
And curfe the breath which keeps him from his own.
E'er fwell the violet's fweets, the rofes bloom,
'Tis well, if fuch a father fcapes the tomb,
With fome kind antidote's protective art,
Ye tyrants, and ye mifers, fteel your heart.

Yet will my friend, while blefs'd with leifure, range,
And view that raree-fhow of wealth the Change?
From fide to fide where gape the harpy-rout,
To purchafe ftocks with money, or without;
No matter which, for 'tis of late the fame,
And dulleft citizens can play the game;
Can, by low arts an ufelefs hoard t' encreafe,
Curfe us with war, or comfort us with peace;
Can fometimes, fo complete the juggler's pow'r,
Make themfelves rich and poor in half-an-hour:
Such turns in ev'ry ftation we behold !
So topfy-turvy run the fchemes of gold !

Can man, vain wretch, furvey with fmiling view
The little infant childifh cares purfue,
Difdainful innocency's fport behold;
While fetter'd in the bafelefs toils of gold,
He mounts the giddy fhip with headftrong mind,
Infulted victim of the feas and wind?
No dangers threat the child's unthinking play,
Urg'd by no curs'd defires their bofoms ftray;

We

We view the follies of their fouls within,
How elfe unlike thee, for they know no fin ?

See the fill'd haven fmiles ; the freighted fhip,
And breathing zephyrs beckon to the **deep** ;
Like daring Raleigh tempt the luring main,
Where India's riches fwell the pride of Spain ;
Or with bold Clive's undaunted bofom fhow'r
Thy terrors 'gainft the throne of hoftil pow'r.
For gold alone ye hear the tempefts fly,
For gold alone ye feek the diftant fky ;
From fcenes of blifs, of eafe, of plenty roam,
To hug, not honor, but your wealth at home.

" Yet, Cenfor, whence this daring rage at ME ?
" What other mortals breathe from madnefs free ?
" The foul of grandeur on the chair of ftate
" Shakes at each chilling blaft of adverfe fate,
" Nor dares one upftart fon of wealth offend,
" But fears to make a foe of ev'ry friend.
" There are, who frantic in a faithlefs dream
" Tread the dark veil and folitary ftream ;
" Pale with affright they rufh in confcious dread,
" And tremble left a wife or fon be dead."

Eternal horrors fhake the mifer's breaft,
No foothing flumbers fan his foul to reft ;

His

His thoughts long vigils fix'd on profit keep,
Tho' death frown o'er him thro' the stormy deep.
But see ! the tempest low'rs, the lightnings fly,
A weight of clouds o'erspreads the loaded sky ;
Away, cries av'rice, hence unmanly fears,
What shudder, dastards, when a cloud appears !
Loose to the main, alas ! this gloomy hour
Is but the signal of a vernal show'r.
When lo ! refounding at the dead of night
Their shudd'ring souls the roaring thunders fright ;
The hoarded treasure hurry'd by the wave
Sinks in the horrors of a watry grave.
Behold him shiv'ring on the shore display'd,
In black affliction's tatter'd garb array'd ;
There fix'd with sighs the letter'd picture shew,
Which paints to charity the tale of woe.—
Fond fool ! in vain pursuits to waste the breath,
Which gain'd are mis'ry, and when lost are death.

Half-willing Hopkins' smiles his friend invite
To pass in social chat the tedious night ;
Rais'd by the narrow stairs enlighten'd round,
Wrap'd in a garret's gloom the wretch he found ;
One chair, one table were his scanty store,
His coat all colors, and his bed the floor ;
One dirty rush-light wink'd its half-clos'd eye,
Which wasted soon can scarce dim light supply :

Sa.]

Sad Hopkins' looks the fading luftre mark,
" Friend, 'tis as well, converfe we in the dark."

   Juft paufe o'er Henry on the bed of death,
What pangs of confcience gnaw his parting breath !
How with a figh the proftrate king furveys
The bold oppreffions of his profp'rous days !
While Empfon's deeds in doubled horrors rife,
And favage Dudley frowns before his eyes;
(Who fcorn'd like Galba to RESIGN command,
To ftab fecurely by another's hand)
Sick of the throne he loaths th' exalted ftate,
Which rules o'er empires with a People's Hate.

   Prudence, thy fmiles we fpurn, and (frantic pride !)
We take the phantom fortune for our guide:
Who finds the ftream with raging thirft opprefs'd,
Whofe home-fpread board regales his hungry breaft,
Whofe plain-fpun veftment fhields his tender frame
From chilling winter, and the fummer's flame,
Whofe garden fheds its variegated fmile,
To fill the lagging hours with honeft toil,
Whofe well-thatch'd cot affords a fafe retreat,
Humbly adorn'd, inelegantly neat,
On HIM kind Heav'n has fhow'r'd its richeft ftore;
Confult fair wifdom, fhe will afk no more.

Perhaps

Perhaps the ſtrain in reaſon's narrow bounds
Coops the free ſpirit from ambition's ſounds;
On then, Licinius, with impatient wing
To grandeur's tow'ring ſeat triumphant ſpring;
Hark! glory calls thee, vault into the car,
Pluck from the throne the ribbon and the ſtar.
If yet repeated tides of treaſure roll,
Nor fill the wiſhes of thy craving ſoul,
Licinius reſtleſs as the queen will tow'r,
Who ting'd with vanities the blaze of pow'r;
Whoſe vengeance bad ſevereſt ſtorms await
Th' unhappy idol of her heart and ſtate;
Bad him ev'n honor's ſacred laws offend,
Revoke his mandate, and diſclaim his Friend.

THE

THE

FIFTEENTH SATIRE

IMITATED.

FIRST-born of reafon, blefs'd religion, hail!
Stamp'd on the foul whofe facred charms prevail;
To ALL the knowledge of a God is given,
Tho' in fantaftic forms man worfhip Heaven.

The darken'd Arabs, who from folly draw
The rambling precepts of their prophet's law,
Tho' fix'd by Mahomet's enflaving nod,
Still, ftill are confcious of a ruling God;
Who gave his much-lov'd prieft celeftial birth,
To fcatter peace and knowledge o'er the earth.
There are, who rev'ling in a holy treat,
Fondly adore the very god they eat;

There

There are, whofe fouls in brutal worfhip ftray,
And hurl their infants to the godhead's prey;
Miftaken fiends, who from their maker's breaft
The richeft virtue of a ruler wreft;
Who think, difdainful of creation's good,
Kind Heav'n can riot in its childrens' blood.

Yet hold, fond flaves, let reafon's fmiles affuage
The guilty tranfports of devotion's rage;
(That rage which never with her charms can fuit,
But finks proud manhood to the grov'ling brute)
Left Heav'n infulted rife in frowning ire,
And o'er your kingdoms pour vindictive fire;
Left wafteful pefts your fruitful verdure fpoil,
Or deluge drown ye from encircling Nile.

But fooner far a foe to fhamelefs art,
Will Gallia prove ftrict honefty at heart;
Sooner refign without a parting groan
The realms which conqueft claims for England's own;
Nor view our Indian ftates with jealous eye,
Fix'd by a fcribled treaty's paper tie.
Ah! rather, England, from experience know
Tho' link'd in friendfhip France is ftill a foe;
Remember, Dunkirk's forfeit pride ye mourn,
Honor their laughter, and their oaths their fcorn;
Remember Dunkirk, nor unheedful yield
To fmooth-tongu'd fraud the triumphs of the field.

Survey

Survey the world from nature's earlieſt prime,
From Eve's tranſgreſſion to the preſent time;
'Midſt all the glaring ſins which ſtain mankind,
Few a whole ſtate's united fault we find;
In moſt, tho' cenſur'd in a people's name,
A king, or fav'rite miniſter's to blame.
Ev'n now there glows in this revolving age
An animated monarch's guilty rage,
'Gainſt thee, Religion, aims its threat'ning fall,
Urg'd by ambition's unrelenting call:
When the loud din of death-reſounding arms
O'erſpread the plains of Auſtria with alarms,
Sighing ſhe ſued in mis'ry's ſofteſt ſtrains,
The Britiſh ſword to ſave her ſinking plains;
Britannia heard; the raging tumults ceaſe,
And jarring nations drop to willing peace.
But glutted now with union's gentler ſounds
She burſts the barriers, and o'erleaps the mounds;
Ev'n wakes her late preſerver's injur'd head,
To arm againſt the kingdom once ſhe fled.

What tho' a ſavage king's inhuman reign
Spreads deſolation o'er the Turkiſh plain;
Yet fiercer far the bloody thoughts which fill
The ranc'rous ardor of the Jeſuits' will.
Fir'd by their brutal lords' impatient might,
Tho' realms involv'd in ign'rance and in night,

The

The flavish herd th' unchriftian doctrines roar,
And to the murd'rer fmooth the fool before.

    Should fome be deaf, whofe animated clay
Springs with the glow of reafon's purer ray,
The feftal dance the holy knaves prepare,
To lull their bofoms from feverer care ;
Soft mufic's voice, the ointment's rich perfume,
The fragrant chaplet's variegated bloom,
Spread their lov'd fweets ; while rev'ling in delight
The day they riot, and they dance the night.

    But now (inhuman fhame !) the trumpet's breath
Wakes into life each inftrument of death ;
Urg'd by the frenzy of religion's force
The thirfty ponyard drives its ruthlefs courfe;
The fons of pride, nor fex, nor weaker age
From fcenes of blood can foften or affuage ;
The rev'rend fenior, and the faithful dame,
And ftripling, perifh in th' unpitying flame.
Some, whofe more haplefs fate with dregs of life
To fcape the fury of th' ungen'rous ftrife,
With half-fhap'd members wander from their home,
And point the crimes of unrelenting Rome.

    Yet thefe are errors grac'd with mercy's fmile,
To fuch whofe rage would defolate an ifle ;

To

To fuch, proud wretches, whofe impatient pow'r
Would thin, like pefts, a nation in an hour:
If one, they cry, the paths of fafety find,
The half of dear revenge is ftill behind.
Fruitlefs refiftance, vain the wheedling arts,
Where cunning prompts, and vengeance fteels their hearts;
Arm'd with thefe bulwarks ev'n their ftriplings laugh
At the weak pow'rs of a Goliah's ftaff.

View now the vaffals of their favage rule,
And drop the villain to furvey the fool;
Knav'ry's fond dupes, felected from the train,
Roam in religion's caufe to India's plain;
There rear the mimic crucifix on high,
GEWGAW fcarce known beneath a diftant fky;
Difplay the polifh'd idol's iv'ry fhow,
And wonder Savages difdain to bow.
Yet ftill difdain they dare, and warm'd to ire
Fly 'gainft the prieft with animated fire;
Tear the fcorn'd folly from his trembling hand,
And ftretch the WILLING Martyr on the fand.

Now fink the crafts of Rome, the rigid face,
And all the barb'rous Jefuits' ftern grimace,
Low'r to the view, while crouds with laughing breaft
Gaze on enraptur'd, and provoke the jeft.

Yet,

Yet, yet exult, 'tis well th' unpolifh'd foul
Some fparks of heav'n-born charity control;
'Tis well fufficient fuch revenge they find,
(Softnefs ne'er center'd in a Jefuit's mind)
Like you, they know not others' breafts to fhake
With horror's engines, with the wheel and ftake;
With pond'rous weights to ftretch the tortur'd limb,
Pour in the open'd heart the boiling ftream;
Like you to fix the flame's relentlefs heat,
And tear the entrails from their vital feat.
Let them rage on; ev'n rev'ling in their blood
Let them in tranfport quaff the purple flood;
Scalp the warm brain, hang o'er each ecchoing groan—
Then fay their rage is pity to your own.

To damp the Proteftant's afpiring arms,
When haughty Gallia fpreads the dire alarms,
She thrids each thrilling nerve of pain and fmart,
A paffage forcing to th' unyielding heart;
Detefted bigot, whofe rapacious foul
No tears can footh, no innocence control.
The tender mother at th' inhuman fire
Sees one by one her little brood expire;
In vain they fhudd'ring clafp the parent's knee,
In vain they fhriek religion's brands to fee;
A long farewel fhe takes with heaving fighs,
And " Now be piteous once—flay me," fhe cries;

" Yes,

" Yes, flay a childlefs, hopelefs wretch, and know
" At once ye rid me of the world and woe."
Look down, aufpicious Heav'n, with tender eye,
Nor fpurn thy injur'd people's eager cry;
Attend their vows, attend their dying groan,
And claim the Chriftian fuff'rer for thine own.

Far better truths thy facred influence draws
To guide the bofom to religion's laws;
Thefe high in glory's richeft fplendors reign,
And beam o'er diftant India's favage plain;
Thefe ftring with ten-fold rage the Pruffian arm,
And on the foes of virtue fpread th' alarm;
Enflam'd by England's gen'rous aid they fly,
Nor in the caufe of virtue fear to die;
One warrior-foul embattled hofts defies,
Tho' a whole Continent againft him rife.

Hail, conqu'ring Fred'ric, whofe immortal praife
The fons of verfe and fons of juftice raife !
Whofe pious arms repeated conquefts blefs,
Great ev'n in ill, and glorious from diftrefs.
What tho' th' unwieldy Ruffian's boafting hand
With favage venom menaces thy land,
Ruffia, whofe troops in weak attempts advance,
The dupes of Auftria, and the fport of France;
What tho' in vengeance of a bigot caufe
They fpurn humanity's ferener laws;

With

With thirſt of ſlaughter vainly they purſue
The ſouls who dare pay homage, where 'tis due;
Vainly they thunder in embattled ire,
The ſov'reign's nod forbids the guilty fire;
The ſov'reign to the ſtate's diſgrace who bleeds,
While bent to poliſh brutes to glory's deeds.

Aſk of the Indian, who at hoſtil hearts
Sharpens the knife, and hurls the pointed darts,
Aſk why with ruthleſs breaſt he aims the blow;
It is not at the Chriſtian, but the foe.
A flow'ry Paradiſe he ſeeks above,
The long'd for realms of laughter and of love;
For light canoes he ſpurns the warring ſhip,
And leaves the poliſh'd world the labors of the deep.
Bluſh, bluſh, ye civiliz'd, and learn to prize
Th' inferior crimes of wretches ye deſpiſe;
No more aſtoniſh'd at th' inglorious might,
Which ſprings alone from ign'rance of the right.

Hail, meek-ey'd charity, thou faireſt teſt
Of god-like greatneſs in the human breaſt!
When friendſhip mourns, thy tender footſteps fly
To ſtill her ſorrows, and allay her ſigh.
When orphans groan beneath th' ungen'rous art,
And the mean harſhneſs of a guardian's heart,
The blooming youths, whoſe long-diſhevel'd hair
Flows the ſoft rival of the lovely fair,

Pitying

Pitying thou still'ft meek innocency's moan,
As if an infult to thyfelf alone.

Can Nature view, nor drop the friendly tear,
The virgin clos'd in her untimely bier ?
Survey the little infant's haplefs doom,
Scarce known to life, and hurry'd to the tomb ?
No, Heav'n-born charity, thy blefs'd control
Will thaw the froft that binds the ftubborn foul ;
Light in the darken'd breaft religion's flame,
And teach him whence he takes the Chriftian's name.
Shall Heav'n-born man, on whofe exalted breaft
Her living fignet reafon has imprefs'd,
Shall Man in error's mazy lab'rinth range,
Slave of caprice, of vanity, and change ?
Full o'er creation's bounds with feraph-wing,
Thou, tow'ring foul, with native ardor fpring ;
Speed thy bold flight to virtue's arduous road,
Spurn the low brute, and mount into the God.

To feel the glow of friendfhip, and to grant
Indulgent fuccor to another's want,
To give content from difcontent to fpring,
O'er fcatter'd ftates to fix a virtuous king,
To hand by gen'rous deeds to diftant fame
The blamelefs glories of a grandfire's name,
To view the world with mercy's fofter eye
Link'd in fociety's eternal tie,

For

For THIS rofe man in Heav'n-defcended birth,
To fill with lordly line the fubject-earth.
But now how vary'd ! in diforder hurl'd
What jarring horrors fhake the frighted world !
The fcene of woe let candid reafon fcan,
She'll cry, that man's the verieft curfe of man.

    Come forth, afpiring foul, to wifdom's fchool,
Fav'rite of reafon, and yet folly's fool ;
Come forth, and dumb irrationals fhall teach,
Low brutes inftruct thee, and the reptil preach.
Afk of the lion, has his lordly rage
The date e'er fhorten'd of a lion's age ?
—From the fame ftock he feels each brother fprings
To form one mighty family of kings.
Yet lower fink ; did ever worm expire
Crufh'd by a fellow reptil's famifh'd ire ?
The worm, which thrives from kindred vengeance free,
The worm, which fattens from the fpoil of thee.

    While man, invidious of another's breath,
Sharpens each iron inftrument of death ;
'Tis not enough for labor's honeft ufe
The toiling rake and plough-fhare to produce ;
To mould the fword their reftlefs hands engage,
And crown with fin's worft deed a fhamelefs rage.

But

But what are thefe ? behold by kindred ire
The brother, father, and the fon expire ;
Their groans they hail, they triumph in their fmart,
And with a glut of vengeance cloy the heart.
But fay, ye Chriftian fouls, whofe gen'rous thought
Beams with the precepts which your favior taught,
Can ye behold the daring frowns of fin,
Nor feel humanity enrag'd within ?
Ye, whom a heav'nly mafter taught to fhew
To pride compaffion, mildnefs to a foe ?

THE

THE

SIXTEENTH SATIRE

IMITATED*.

FIVE pounds *per* man ! the bleffings, friend, how
  great
  Which gen'rous ardor fhow'rs on Britain's ftate !
Ye fons of war, infpir'd by falfe alarms
No more we fhudder at the din of arms ;
Sure of fuccefs ye tread th' embattled ftrand,
When wealth's rich bounties brace the warrior's hand.

---

* The following imitation turns upon the late lord lieutenant of Middlefex's having declined to adhere to the meafures prefcribed by an act of
parliament for the promotion of that falutary eftablifhment the militia,
and encouraging a fubfcription for raifing foldiers by ONE of his own ;
on which occafion a fplendid meeting was held at the St. Albans tavern,
Pall Mall, as feveral were afterwards at the celebrated captain Lamb's
auction-room for the militia itfelf.

Q   From

From you, ye lib'ral, heav'nly tranſports ſpring,
A noble's ſelf applauds you to the king;
Ye bid the triumphs of the long-mourn'd field
To ocean's conqu'ring pride no longer yield.

    Let other eyes with faſcinated view
The poor militia's uſeleſs charms purſue;
We know far better ſhields—the herd diſdain,
Back to their homes expel the abject train;
Alas! difus'd to war's tremendous ſhew,
Their ſouls will never dare to face a foe;
Their country's call but whiſtles to the air,
Unknown the chaplain's, and the ſurgeon's care.
Ev'n from their breaſts the clowniſh ruſt to ſhake,
The warrior's leſſon from yourſelves they take;
Loud-ſtamp in hob-nail'd ſhoes with mimic might,
And ſummon'd to the left-hand ſeek the right.

    Lo! while the regulars' bright ſtandards fly
Round well-form'd troops beneath Germania's ſky,
Ne'er from their kingdom's bounds theſe heroes roam,
At beſt but for a trifle doom'd from home;
Well, well ye know them, with ſuperior ſmile
Ye eye their marches, and deride their toil.
Dare they th' affront return?—their rage ye drown
With one grim look, and blaſt them at a frown;
While thro' each rank 'the ſcoffing taunts ye ſhow'r,
And pity England arm'd with ſuch a pow'r.

Rail

Rail on, protectors, in a carelefs eafe,
Th' infulting ftrain refent they as they pleafe;
Apply they to the law? ye ftill are free;
Poor fools! no council pleads without a fee:
Not honeft Verres would for such declaim,
Meek Verres of difinterefted fame.

Go, with whole bones contentedly retire,
Nor roufe a regular's experienc'd fire;
The wretched prifons they have fill'd defend,
They—brave in arms, and heroes to the end—
Few free-born vot'ries a militia proves,
No army but his own a ftatefman loves.

Dry, dry your tears, left to the ferjeant fent
You're whip'd, vile mifcreant, thro' the regiment;
A wretch who dares complain; the foldiers cry;
Go now once more, and falter out a lie.
No fcruples croud a camp; ev'n boldly fhew
The wound they gave you, they difclaim the blow.
Amid the motley tribe the fame thy lot,
Th' intrepid Irifhman, or hungry Scot;
Not ev'n the fanguin Welch a friend will fhield
Againft their mighty brethren of the field.

Should rapine's fons lay wafte my fertil grounds,
Or move my landmark from its ancient bounds,

Whofe

Whofe ftone has fix'd with ftamp ferene and clear
Th' undoubted portion of five hundred year;
Or fhould the wretches view with ftedfaft eyes
The loan entrufted, and forfwear the prize;
Tho' the full witnefs prove the well-known hand,
Ere law's redrefs ye feek, with paufes ftand.
Year rolls on year when once the fuit's begun,
Term after term fucceeds, and nothing done;
Delays in crouds reftrain the courfe of right,
And knotty quirks elude the gazing fight.
This to the low'r of wifdom pulls his face,
This with foft-waving arm debates the cafe;
This pumps out founds with meditation deep,
To lull with fpecious phrafe his client's fleep—
Yet rather, friend, reftrain thy raging breaft,
One half the claim refign to fave the reft.

Warriors far fooner end the dreadful ftrife,
The fword's more honor'd conteft ends their life;
Hint but th' affront, the ready champion draws,
Nor feeks the ling'ring peril of the laws.

The ftripling hurry'd to his fire's abode
Quits for the manly fword the infant rod;
To him no riches fortune's fmiles have blown,
So on the hero flies to feek his own.
The fcorn'd militia's fons at plenty's board
The focial converfe leave to grafp the fword,

Britannia's

Britannia's wants with ardent fire behold,
Nor feek to fpeed their fteps their country's gold.
Thee joys ferener, Middlefex, await,
Thy purfe befpeaks thee fervant of the ftate;
Let other faces feel the vulgar fcar,
It is not thine to tremble at a war.

But you, ye fquadrons, fan the ftatefman's flame,
Go, fpread the terrors of your country's fame;
So may applaufe your gen'rous labors crown;—
In three fhort years adorn'd with juft renown
So may your fouls each laurel'd glory fee,
Lords of yourfelves, and of the CITY free.
There fwell'd with pride behind the counter ftand,
Retailing nick-nacks with induftrious hand;
There truly great, tho' votelefs, you may reign,
GREAT AS THE BLACKSMITH-DUKE OF AQUITAIN.